# A DAY IN THE LIFE OF...

## CREATIVE WRITING FROM THE WEST MIDLANDS 2001

Edited by Dave Thomas

First published in Great Britain in 2001 by
*YOUNG WRITERS*
Remus House,
Coltsfoot Drive,
Peterborough, PE2 9JX
Telephone (01733) 890066

All Rights Reserved

*Copyright Contributors 2000*

HB ISBN 0 75432 362 5
SB ISBN 0 75432 363 3

# *FOREWORD*

This year, Young Writers proudly presents a showcase of the best 'A Day In The Life Of . . .' short stories, from up-and-coming writers nationwide.

To write a short story is a difficult exercise. Much imagination and skill is required. *A Day In The Life Of . . . Creative Writing From The West Midlands 2001,* achieves and exceeds these requirements. This exciting anthology will not disappoint the reader.

The thought, effort, imagination and hard work put into each story impressed us all, and again, the task of editing proved demanding due to the quality of entries received, but was nevertheless enjoyable.

We hope you are as pleased as we are with the final selection and that you continue to enjoy *A Day In The Life Of . . . Creative Writing From The West Midlands 2001* for many years to come.

# CONTENTS

Beacon Primary School
| | | |
|---|---|---|
| | Sally Webb | 1 |
| | Adrian Daker | 2 |
| | Emma Watabiki | 3 |
| | Sam Wilson | 4 |
| | Jamie Lilgallon | 5 |
| | Natalie Wilcox | 6 |
| | Aaron Webb | 8 |
| | Christopher Bayliss | 9 |
| | Kerry-Ann Stone | 10 |
| | Nicky Wall | 11 |
| | Nichola Haddon | 12 |
| | Jodie Rowlands | 13 |
| | Laura Allkins | 14 |
| | Rosie Higham | 15 |
| | David Gatenby | 16 |
| | Edward Wilson | 17 |
| | Frances Mills | 18 |
| | Amie Quinn | 19 |
| | Sarah Broomhall | 20 |
| | Charlotte Wood | 21 |
| | James Broomhall | 22 |
| | Jade Evans | 23 |
| | K'Lee Green | 24 |

Birchills CE Primary Community School
| | | |
|---|---|---|
| | Daniel Orton | 25 |

Dorridge Junior School
| | | |
|---|---|---|
| | Hannah Train | 26 |
| | Katie Purser | 27 |
| | Abigail Waters | 28 |
| | Jennifer Hall | 29 |
| | Laura Baker | 30 |
| | Claire Tolley | 31 |
| | Jennifer Blackhall | 32 |

|  |  |
|---|---|
| Hayley Wallwork | 33 |
| Elizabeth Pratt | 34 |

**Eversfield Preparatory School**

|  |  |
|---|---|
| James Bowser | 35 |
| William Chamberlain | 36 |
| Sam Jamison | 37 |
| Oliver Lowson | 38 |
| Elliot Mintz | 39 |
| Matthew Simpson | 40 |
| Ben Taylor | 41 |
| Edmund Westlake | 42 |
| Simon Barley | 43 |
| David Cross | 44 |
| Joe White | 45 |

**Four Oaks Junior School**

|  |  |
|---|---|
| Isabel Richards | 46 |
| James Hughes | 47 |
| Billy McGrail | 48 |
| Daniel Longmore | 49 |
| Sam Parsons | 50 |
| Emily Jackson | 51 |
| Robert Stainforth | 52 |
| Samantha Hough | 53 |
| Samuel Hepburn | 54 |
| Liam Woods | 55 |
| Adam Moore | 56 |
| Chris Cutler | 57 |
| Seth Taylor | 58 |
| James Pope | 59 |
| Charlotte Smith | 60 |
| Natasha Emmerson | 61 |
| Rebecca Amyes | 62 |
| Steven Rowley | 63 |
| Rachel Feasey | 64 |
| Bradley McDowall | 65 |

George Betts Primary School
- Dominique Paisley — 66
- Syria Ewers — 67
- Manjinder Dhesi — 68

Grove Vale Primary School
- William Reynolds — 69
- Carl Tinsley — 70
- Adam Dodd — 71
- Adam Oggelsby — 72
- Carly Woakes — 73
- Thomas Niblett — 74
- Sanchez Chatha — 75

King Edward VI Camp Hill School For Girls
- Naomi Shipman — 76
- Louisa Ball — 77
- Emma Matthews — 78
- Amy Winchester — 79
- Kate Wilson — 80
- Miriam Toolan — 81
- Hannah Slade — 82
- Anna Pugh — 84
- Abigail Jennings — 85
- Tara Curzon — 86
- Kirsty McGuff — 87
- Leigh Salsbury — 88
- Emily Johnson — 89
- Lucy Scholes — 90
- Genevieve Ewing — 91
- Shivani Shah — 92
- Shivani Tandon — 93
- Faiza Fazal — 94
- Chrissy Wong — 95
- Bushra Jahangir — 96
- Laura J Davies — 97
- Sema Latif — 98
- Parul Kenth — 99

Manor Primary School
    Christina Cheung — 100

Moor Green Junior School
    Sophia Hamid — 101
    Tara Roleston — 102
    Olivia Sutton — 103
    Loretta Cummins — 104
    Louise E Langan — 105
    Kieran Conlon — 106
    Jasmine Fennell — 107
    Abeeda Pasha — 108
    Wasim Hussain — 110
    Kay Wilson — 111
    Stacey Rhodes — 112
    Hayley Sanders — 113
    Kerrie Fox — 114
    Billy Woodhurst — 115
    Kerry Doak — 116
    Inderjit Ramm — 117
    Lisa Titshall — 118
    Emma Thorpe — 119
    Roxanne Ali — 120
    Leanne Jones — 121
    Aisha Malik — 122
    Aaron Lammy — 123
    Karanvir Shergill — 124
    Christopher Gumbley — 125
    Danielle Rhodes — 126
    Wayne McVeigh — 127

St John Fisher RC Primary School, Coventry
    Kieran Davis — 128
    Laura McGrath — 129
    Ryan Gillespie — 130
    Phillip Hall — 131
    Liam Jordan — 132
    Luke McAleer — 133

|  |  |
|---|---|
| Richard Taylor | 134 |
| Sinead Docherty | 135 |
| Jolee Gavin | 136 |
| Nicola Gormley | 137 |
| Natalia Costa | 138 |

Yarnfield Primary School

|  |  |
|---|---|
| Luke Southan | 139 |
| Aliasgher Hassam | 140 |
| Katie Turner | 141 |
| Toni Lee | 142 |
| Emma Sloggie | 143 |
| Mark Butler | 144 |
| Sam Slattery | 145 |
| Aileen Brady | 146 |
| Aaron Evans | 147 |
| Jason Bassett | 148 |
| Sireena Bibi | 149 |
| Kirsty Meddings | 150 |
| Adam Curtis | 151 |
| Narinderpal Singh | 152 |
| Liam Jelfs | 153 |
| Adam Brinkworth | 154 |
| Emma O'Neill | 155 |
| Craig Jelley | 156 |
| Belinda Forde | 157 |
| Robert Harper | 158 |
| Shahara Choudhury | 159 |
| Vicky Sheridan | 160 |
| Cherrelle Foster | 163 |

*The Stories*

# A Day In The Life Of A Chair

So peaceful, so quiet, so . . . childless.
Oh no, here we go again, I can hear them hurtling towards me, thundering up the corridors, waiting for the kill. Oh please be a sensible one. Here goes . . . Oh, my god! . . . Aaahhh! Oh no! It's a fat one! What am I going to do? Hang on a minute, would you put me down on all fours please. Excuse me! Wooh! Woah! . . . Ouch!

Silly children. Phew! He's going, it's all change for the next lesson, well hooray for that.

Do, doo, do! Yes, a sensible one finally heading for me. Hang on, wait a minute, where am I going? Oh, I forgot it was the meningitis jab today I've got to have my jab too I think. Why, may I ask am I just sitting here with nobody on me. I can't believe it, a repeat of yesterday ha!! Wait a minute, I can hear them now they sound a bit excited about this jab. Oh well, here comes my first customer. That's a first, she is actually sitting still, finally I can relax.

I'm on my way back to the classroom. Is there a riot or something? Oh, it's just dinner time.

Some time alone at last. Here they come, running, screaming, shouting, walking and laughing all at the same time - amazing!

I'm absolutely freezing. Aaagh peace and quiet.

Assembly time. School's finished.

*Sally Webb (10)*
*Beacon Primary School*

## A Day In The Life Of Test

Today is special for me, I'm challenging the Big Boss Man for his hardcore belt, but first I've got to find some weapons to use. But anyway, Big Boss Man might crack me over the head with his knife-stick.

Oh no! Me and Albert have got a tag-team match against the Dudley Boys in ten minutes. Knock, knock! 'Hi Test it's me D'Von, we want to call the match off.'

Yes! Now I can watch all the other matches which are going on . . . Oh no! Trish is fighting Tori. No! Trish my manager has just been power-bombed through a table by Bubah-Ray Dudley . . . Yes the Rock is fighting Triple H for the WWF Champion's belt. Yes! Go on Rock win. Yes! . . . Well done . . . No! The Rock can't be disqualified!

'I wonder what Big Boss Man's doing, I've got to fight him in about 25 minutes, I'm going for a drink Jeff. I'm back and ready for the match!'

My music comes on and then I was petrified when the Big Boss Man's music was playing. The bell went and then we were wrestling and when I got him to the ground. I got out a weapon, but before I could hit him with it - crack! He hit me over the head with a bin. Then he stood me up in the corner where I DDT'ed him and hit him in the belly and I won his belt.

*Adrian Daker (11)*
*Beacon Primary School*

## A Day In The Life Of An Air Stewardess

It was Friday and I was flying to Paris, it wasn't a long flight but I didn't want to go.

I put my uniform on and said goodbye to my mum and off I went to Birmingham Airport, my day had begun.

When I arrived, it seemed dull and gloomy, not a nice day, but when I got through the doors it seemed to brighten up.

I got to the check-in desk and my friend who was on check-in said 'Hello!' and that made it even brighter.

It was noon and I could hear businessmen and not many, just a few holidaymakers coming towards me. Putting on a smile I started to greet the passengers.

Not long before it was take off, another girl shut the door while I checked seat belts. The rumbling of the engines signalled we were on the runway and then high in the sky. We made a successful take off.

During the flight I gave out drinks, not any meals - not on a short flight. Just then, the drinks trolley fell over and we realised a bolt of lightning had struck the plane.

The captain said not to panic, and soon we landed.

We didn't take passengers back, it would be too dangerous. So it wasn't such a bad day after all.

*Emma Watabiki (11)*
*Beacon Primary School*

# A Day In The Life Of Albert Einstein

I had a very interesting day I tried and tested my latest formula - my Theory of Relativity you see!

I got up this morning by the sound of the alarm clock which I had bought for my birthday. I decided to go to bed as it was Saturday. After that I did manage to get up at about 10 o'clock, I had a lot to do that day. I had breakfast, I can't remember what I had, but so what!

I went into my laboratory to test my new formula because I was giving a presentation that afternoon. I sat down at my computer and started to write my presentation. I sat writing for about an hour. It started to get boring so I stopped and had coffee and my pipe.

I had to carry on as my presentation was at eight o'clock so I had to get a move on. I was presenting it to the Science Institute in London.

It was time the limo came to pick me up, I thought about it and all the best scientists would be there. I arrived, I had a red carpet waiting for me and as I opened the door I heard all of my fans cheering. I was in my best dinner suit.

I walked up onto the stage and saw all the people. There was the head of NASA and the Queen and loads of other very important people. I started and they seemed very impressed by what I'd said. In the end they cheered and clapped, I was very pleased.

*Sam Wilson (11)*
*Beacon Primary School*

## A Day In The Life Of Socko

As I walked down the ramp I knew I could feel it, I was the proudest thing in the world being on Mankind's hand.

I will hold onto the cell as Mankind steps in, we will hear the Undertaker's dreaded music as he comes down with Paul Bearer. I knew Mankind was full of fear and so was I for that matter.

The whole place went black and then I dropped, dropped onto the floor, still holding onto Mankind's hand. The lights came back on, Mankind's head was lifted and I couldn't stand it any longer, I pounded at his chest as quick as lightning I went down and a jab upwards sent him dazed.

I ran him into the corner as I grabbed his head and smashed it off the turnbuckle and threw him into Paul Bearer. Mankind climbed out and put Undertaker onto the anouncer's table. It was time - I flew into his mouth and pulled his tongue, then I came out and flung my arm across Paul Bearer's chest.

I had the Undertaker on the top of the cell, I grabbed his arms and did the double-arm DDT onto the steel.

I knocked him through the gap in the top of the cell as Mankind got ready for his famous leg drop. Music came on, my worst enemy's music came on, Vince and his son Shane McMahon. I pulled Mankind as me and the other hand did a double clothesline. I picked up a chair and gave Paul Bearer a quick crack over the head, I pulled Mankind back into the cell and set the chair up and then grabbed Undertaker's legs as we piledrived him onto it.

Mankind gets the cover, will we win? 1 . . . 2 . . . 3 . . . We've won! I hold the belt in joy as we go backstage to celebrate with our new companion The Heavyweight Title.

*Jamie Lilgallon (11)*
*Beacon Primary School*

# A Day In The Life Of Dennis 'Worm' Rodman

Dring! Dring! Dring - bleep! 'Oh no! Training starts in fifteen minutes.'
'Dennis, breakfast is ready' called Jeffery from two floors down.
'Okay Jeffery, I'm coming down now.'

I ran downstairs as fast as I could. Downstairs I grabbed my training bag and some toast, ran out the door and ran to training.

'You only just got here!' shouted the Coach.
'Sorry I'm late Coach,' I said.
'Okay, just make sure you're on time tomorrow Dennis!'

Later . . .

'Okay, let's get those legs up. Come on, ten miles, don't stop!'
Oh well, only another half an hour to go.
'Dennis, stop daydreaming,' Coach shouted.
'Sorry Coach!' I said back.
'Training has finished,' Coach said 'remember it's the big match tonight.'
'Yes boss!' We all said.
'Listen up, we're here, we can't turn back,' the Coach said happily, trying to cheer us up.
'You can't cheer us up Coach!' Pippen said gloomily.
'Yeah because you can't cheer up very much when you're playing the Miami Dolphins.' Kukoc said.
'Just get out there and win!'

'Hello and welcome to Chicago where the Chicago Bulls face the Miami Dolphins . . . and it's off . . . the Chicago Bulls have possession . . . Pippen, Rodman, Rodman shoots - he scores. The Chicago Bulls are leading two points to none.

'With one minute to go, Slimson, Jacobs, Jacob scores, it's now forty-two points to thirty-nine and that means the Bulls have won it! Yes, they've won the cup!'

'Yes we've won the cup, well done!' Coach nearly shouted.

'Go home lads. Bye!'

*Natalie Wilcox (10)*
*Beacon Primary School*

# A Day In The Life Of A Coca Cola Bottle

Here I am, a Coca Cola bottle sitting there in the fridge . . . wait! Pick me up, I have been here for weeks . . .
Yes, he's picking me . . . Aw don't throw me into the trolley . . . Yeah we are going to the checkout . . . Aw! That beep hurts my ears. It's all cramped in this bag with the bread and milk . . . Into the car boot we go. This engine sure is noisy, why are we bumping? We must be on those speed bumps, that's why.

I am being carried into the house. No! What's this? All my cola is being drunk . . . Oh, thank you, you've put me down . . . Wait! Where are we going? You're putting me in the smelly, stinky bin . . . Oh, it smells . . . Look at all these potato peelings and empty crisp packets. It looks like we are being taken for a ride . . . We are going to the rubbish lorry . . . Hey, we keep stopping and starting.

'Who are you?'
'Oh, I'm just a Fanta bottle.'
'Well, where are they taking us?'
'They're taking us to the tip where we'll be crushed and flattened.'
'Well, I'm going to the bottom to see if my mates are there.'
'Yeah! Well goodbye!'

'Oh no! I'm going to be crushed.
Here, don't throw me about. It's coming . . .
No! I'm being crushed . . . I'm not going to be seen again!'

*Aaron Webb (11)*
*Beacon Primary School*

## A Day In The Life Of A Steak

A lovely day for me, a cool day in the freezer,
'I'm having a barbecue. Do you want to come? I've got steak.'
My day isn't it? I'm going to be cooked and eaten.
Two hours later, 'I'm down to my last two steaks . . .'
Phew I'm still alive, but I got him in here with me. Fred,
He's the most popular steak in here . . .

Oh no, he's coming in, hold on it's raining. Yes, he can't cook me now
No it's just the h h hose p p pipe, which one is it going to pick?
Supermodel here or me. Yes, he's got supermodel, bye, bye, dipstick.
Now, I've got about another three minutes till he comes and gets me, so
I'll have a three minute rest.

Two and a half minutes later - hold on that was only two and a half minutes rest. You'd better give me another thirty seconds rest. Oh well, I'm just going to have to be cooked now.

'Oh that looks painful Fred!'
'It is!'

Well I'm on next, so I'll have to find out 'Ow ooh ooh ow!
You're right, this is painful and it's burning my precious skin.'
We'll meet . . . Oh no, I'm starting to act like a human.
'You don't want it now? Well make up your mind. Well we'll have it for supper tonight.'

A few hours later, supper time.

'Let's eat our steak while we're watching *You've Been Framed*.
Well my time had to come - bye!

***Christopher Bayliss  (11)***
***Beacon Primary School***

# A Day In The Life Of A Rubber

It's Tuesday morning, I hope Sam isn't coming today because yesterday during the SATs spelling test he was rubbing me away. I was 25cm long before we started the test, now I'm 15cm. He was rubbing and chewing me.

It's two hours until they come. Now I can hear the headmaster putting something on the desk. I'm being picked up, off the floor and . . . phew! I'm being put on the teacher's desk, I thought he was going to put me on Sam's desk.

*One hour later*

Now I can hear the teacher getting ready for the lessons. The bell has rung, I can hear year six saying 'Do we have to come?' Then I can hear the others running into class.

I've spotted Sam, he's at the desk asking something like which test is first, I hope it's Science because Sam won't need me.
'Wait like the rest, now sit down.' Miss Marsh replied.
The children were chatting, but now are in their seats.
'The first test is . . .'
Science, I'm saying to myself.
'First test is Science,' Miss Marsh said.
Yes, I'm not on his desk!
Instead I'm on his brother's desk, who *will* need me for the diagrams. At least he won't *flick me.*

It's home time, it's nice and quiet. I'm lying awake, worrying about who I'll have tomorrow. Well I don't care as long as it's not Sam!

**Kerry-Ann Stone (11)**
**Beacon Primary School**

## A DAY IN THE LIFE OF A FOOTBALL

It was ten minutes away from the FA Cup Final between West Brom and Wolves.

'Imagine someone ten times as big as you, kicking you around,' the football said to himself.
I was a yard away from being belted by the mid-fielder and *bang!* The ball got whacked.
Anyway, I had gone into the net for the first time for West Brom.

I wished somebody had kicked me high into the stadium and the supporters never threw me back . . . but the next thing I knew I was in the net. It was 1 - 1 and the match could go either way.

I was getting scared, I could see the players' faces, both of them ready to lose their tempers.

There were two players coming for me now, one from each team. They both stretched out a leg, I cut back and saw their faces again then . . . the Wolves player cleared me out of play.

'I wish somebody would hurry up and score,' the football said.
The match finished. It was a penalty.

'Penalties last about three to seven minutes,' said the football to himself.

Two penalties had been kicked by each team. Wolves scored two and West Brom hit the bar and missed on their other ball.

West Brom missed their third penalty. Apparently, they belted it over and knocked an Albion fan unconscious.
'Yes, the match has ended,' the football said.

It had ended with Wolves winning the FA Cup and a disappointed, useless West Bromwich Albion going home!

*Nicky Wall (11)*
*Beacon Primary School*

# A Day In The Life Of A Pencil

I'm in school now and I can hear all the doors creaking in the classrooms. Shoes clattering off, the teachers and oh no! The bell's just gone. The children are rushing up the stairs and making a fuss.

The children have just come into the classroom. Who's going to pick me? The girl with the neat writing's coming, she's picked the one behind me. Oh no! The scruffiest boy is coming to pick me up, the one who only does one page a lesson. He's picked me up and gone to sit down.

It's English now and he's got spellings. The teacher's started to shout the spellings out. He's missed about five out so far, and I'm feeling dizzy from all the spinning around.

English is over, and it's maths now, they've got a mental maths test.

He's really good at maths, the maths test is over and he's got dinner now. The dinner bell goes and the fuss all starts again. He starts to draw on wood and then chips it.

I'm feeling sick and he's squeezing me so hard I can hardly breath. It's games now and I've got peace at last. The bell's just gone and I'm put back in the holder.

It's home time, and I'm really tired.

Goodnight!

*Nichola Haddon (11)*
*Beacon Primary School*

## A Day In The Life Of A Pencil

Peace and quiet at last while the children go out to break for about fifteen minutes . . . Oh no, the children are coming in . . . Yes! The neatest writer is coming to pick me up . . . No! It's the untidy person who bites the end of me.

Finally, it's time to go home . . . He's taking me home . . . Oh no! I'll bet you that all day he's going to chew the end of me.

Next break he just thought he'd forgotten to take me to school, the teacher said to him 'Where's your pencil?'
'I left it at home!'
'Well you'd better bring it tomorrow.'

The neatest person who doesn't chew the end of me every day. She didn't take me home, she left me in her pencil case, that's what I'm for.

I was writing when the teacher was talking . . . The teacher took me away . . . She put me on her desk until we had to write, the teacher wrote with me, she has very good handwriting. At home time, she left me in her desk . . . when she came in she picked me up and put me in her bag and took me home.

When she took me home she left me in her bag for about fifteen minutes and she took me out and wrote with me. She was marking, and all I had to write was ticks and crosses. She had to mark maths books, English, science and geography. I was tired.

Finally, I got short - and was thrown away.

*Jodie Rowlands (11)*
*Beacon Primary School*

## A Day In The Life Of A Rubber

I was lying in a shop one Friday morning waiting to be sold, when Lisa (the boss) put a notice on the board outside.

For sale - for more details
ring 0121 632 2247

Oh no! If someone buys this shop I'll be moved away. So Billy struggled his way to the top 'Hey, move!'
'Get lost!' said the other rubbers who were being pushed around.

Some of the rubbers asked Billy why he was moving to the top 'I'm moving to the top because Lisa is selling the shop and I have to be bought so I don't get moved when someone else buys the shop.' explained Billy.

*Bang!* The door flew open and this man walked in.
'Where are the rubbers, lady?'
'Over there,' said Lisa.

As the man came towards Billy and his friends with his big boots on and the moody grin on his face. Billy suddenly realised that he didn't particularly want to go with this man, but before Billy got ready to struggle back down, it was too late.
'This will do,' said the man.

When the man took Billy to the till, Lisa got out a blue bag without any care and she dropped him into it.

Before the man picked up the bag, Billy managed to struggle to the top and fell out of the bag. Later Lisa took him back with his friends.

*Laura Allkins (11)*
*Beacon Primary School*

## A Day In The Life Of A Spoon

I'm going to tell you about my worst day. I was only a little youngster, - why did it have to be me? I mean I'm only a spoon!

Anyway, I woke at the sound of an alarm clock. They're coming, I was at the bottom of the pile. Please pick me for breakfast. I pushed the other spoons out of the way and got to the front. I could hear them run downstairs. A creak - it was the door, then I could see bits of light. They opened the cupboard, I was excited, hoping it was Mel and not Alice. You see Mel's gentle and Alice just isn't!

It opened 'Oh, it's Alice!'
I tried to move back but it was too late she'd got me. 'Be gentle!' I did try to wriggle away but the more I did the harder she gripped. Was she going to kill me?

'Ouch!' She dropped me, she picked me up and swilled me under the tap. *It was cold!* But it was good for my head. She used me for breakfast, it was like a dream, she didn't bang me.

She left me on the side, I thought things would get better, but they didn't.

Mom swilled me under the hot tap, it was like a bath. then she used me for the dog food, it tasted horrible. Afterwards I was put in the dishwasher, then finally it finished, and they put me back.

I was at the bottom, I thought before dropping off, I'm not pushing to the front tomorrow!

*Rosie Higham (11)*
*Beacon Primary School*

## A DAY IN THE LIFE OF STEVE PEAT

It was the day of the Downhill World Championship. I was getting ready for the race, it was about 38°C, it was a good job I had the air conditioning on or I'd probably be toast. It was 6.30am and the race was at 4.00pm so I had plenty of time to get ready.

I went to my garage and there it was a GT 4000. If you think I paid for it, you must be joking!

I sat on it and felt a warm feeling rush through me as the suspension went down. I couldn't stop thinking I'm Steve Peat, the worlds best DH cyclist. I'm going to go out of this house at 3.30pm and win this race.

I pressed the button on my garage door, it opened and I went out and started to do a couple of tricks before I had my breakfast. Even though I was in the States, I had a full English.

About six hours later a large lorry pulled up, it had loads of room to put my bike on.

When I got there, people were holding up banners and cheering me on. *Bang!* The race had started. The first jump was small so I only got a bit of air but Vazauez had come off. He was straight ahead of me. I pedalled as fast as I could and made it.

I'd won! I had won!

*David Gatenby (11)*
*Beacon Primary School*

## A Day In The Life Of A Computer

'Oh no, not again!' he said as he got up. He was thinking about what would happen. Slowly people started to come in, then the first person used him.

'Not word processing!' he said to himself 'Ow, oow, ow, oow don't hit me so hard, that hurts!'

I hope it's not the kid that dribbles over you, it gets right up my chips.

Some dipstick crashed me, so I got booted up again and it hurt! Then to make it better, the same dipstick broke my monitor so I had another new one. I'm getting sick of this, sick of it.

I got a computer bug so some twit rebooted me and I forgot everything including the bosses money file. He didn't lose much anyway.

Someone put me in a box and then into a van. When I came back, I felt a lot better and I had an Internet cam.

We then had a power cut and it all happened so quickly I was off. Then I was back on plus a warning sign *Power Cut Continues!* They clicked OK so I went on.

Loading SIMs, oh I love this playing, shopping and watching people play football but of course it's all virtual. None of it's real, if only it was. I would love to be a human for a day going shopping and playing football. I only hear about it, if only I were human.

Maybe someone will make me into a human one day?

*Edward Wilson (11)*
*Beacon Primary School*

# A Day In The Life Of A Pencil Crayon

8.45am - Here I am lying in the classroom cupboard with these other worthless crayons. I have no idea why the school bought them all, because I am a special crayon. I am gold and cost 75p. I wish I will get chosen several times today. Oh, of course I will because I am a lot better than all those 25p reds and yellows, greens and blues.

*'Stomp, scream, chatter!'* Oh yeah! The kids are coming. I can hear the teacher telling them to settle down.

*What?* A colouring competition. *Wow!* I must prepare myself to be stuck in that sharpener and whizzed around because I am going to be 7cm or even shorter soon.

10.45am - Break time thank goodness. I could go on for ever telling you what I have coloured in today but I only have fifteen minutes to tell you.

11.00am - They are coming back now.

Teacher's voice, 'Back to your colouring children.' Oh no, Jamie Taylor's coming towards the box. No! Don't pick me. Oh he has. The trouble with Jamie is he colours too hard, he has broken lots of crayons including the jumbo extra ones.

I can feel myself cracking. *'Crack, crack, snap!'* He broke me. He broke . . . me!

He's taking me to the teacher. She looks at me and tries to stick me back together with sticky tape, but it won't work. Before I know it I am lying on top of lots of sharpenings in the *bin.*

I'm scared, very scared.

3.30pm - End of school and I'm still in the bottom of this bin. Someone's coming . . . it's the cleaner. She's emptying the bin. Goodbye classroom, I'll miss you.

*Frances Mills (11)*
**Beacon Primary School**

## A Day In The Life Of A Cat

As I wake up I see my brothers and sisters sleeping around me. The pet shop is as quiet as the grave apart from the occasional purr from my brothers and sisters. I stand up on my four legs and go to my bowl and have something to eat.

Then I go back to lying down in the cage. I start to think just how good life is when the door is unlocked and opened. I hear the shopkeeper walking in. She walks up to the cage, my brothers and sisters awake. The shopkeeper lifts me out of the cage and starts stroking my fur softly.

She calls me 'Puss' and I start to wonder why she calls me that, but then I am distracted, the door opens and a very pretty lady walks in, she looks at me with her bright blue eyes.

The next thing I know, I am in a cardboard box alone without knowing when I will see my family again. I feel very sad, but then the box is opened and I see the pretty lady again and I think I am back in the pet shop, but my hopes of going back are destroyed.

I am in a very beautiful room. I know what has happened. I've been bought. I know I will get used to my new home but forever I will long for the day I see my family again.

*Amie Quinn (11)*
*Beacon Primary School*

# A Day In The Life Of A Computer

Here I am waiting to be bought. Someone's coming towards me . . . Are they . . . ? Oh no, they're not. I wish someone would buy me.

Who are they? They look horrible, the boys are whacking each other. Oh no, they're coming towards me. Please, please, please don't buy me. Oh no, it looks as if they already have. Bye store, I'll miss you.

Ow, that hurt! Please go slow over the bumps. Ow, careful, I'm fragile.

Oh no, please help, the boys are coming to open me. Phew their dad has come to do it. Now what's he doing? Oh, he is taking me upstairs *into the boys' room!*

I can hear them coming upstairs now. Thank goodness that their dad locked the door . . . . did he? Oh no! He must have forgotten to. Their dad is switching me on. It looks as though I am working perfectly. 'Boys,' their dad shouted, 'the computer's working.'

Oh no! I thought, they're going to break me. I can hear one of them crying now. The door is opening, they rushed in fighting over the chair. One went back downstairs and the other one started to play the game. Here we go, I wonder what he's going to play? I hope he doesn't play Space Aliens.

Oh I wish I hadn't said that. *Boom! Boom!* the game had started. He decided to get off and go to bed.

All of a sudden it went black. I think he has shut me down . . . yes! Finally some peace.

**Sarah Broomhall (11)**
**Beacon Primary School**

# A Day In The Life Of A Shopping Trolley

'They are going to open soon Rickety.'
'I know, I wonder what sort of people I will get today? Yesterday I got a screaming child sitting in me, an old lady, a lady with 17 kids and a teenager doing the shopping and bumping me every chance he got. You should see the dents. It is my last day today. I hope that someone nice will choose me today.'
The doors opened.
'Mom, that one, that one!'
'No Tim. This one's better,' replied Tim's mom.
It's me!
'Come on Tim.'
Brum, off we go!
'Slow down please,' I said, but of course they couldn't hear me.
I've had a whole hour of racing about and crashing into things now. Luckily my next load is more comfortable. It's an old lady. She's putting some weird things in me. Aarrgghh! False teeth cleaner.
I'm on my next load. No, it's her, she's the one that lets her kids sit in me, *help!*
*Crash!* that's the tenth time I've crashed into the wall of beans. I've got beans all over me. The lady's wiping them off, missing some. I'm at the check-out now. The lady's pushing me into the trolley park.
I've been sitting here ages, it must be closing time.
What's this, a man's pushing me.
*Crash!*
'Clicker! Clanger, you're here.'
This is the park for retired trolleys. I've dreamed of this moment and now I'm here.
*Yippee!*
At last, Clicker was in harmony for the rest of his life, no more crashing, just peace.

***Charlotte Wood (11)***
***Beacon Primary School***

## A Day In The Life Of Hamster

Sleep, sleep and more sleep that's all I do for most of the day. I only get up to eat and drink. Oh no he's coming, it's that kid who likes to torture me, he's picking me up and he's beginning to squeeze me, *'Aarrgh!'*

He's getting tighter, *'Oops,* I need the toilet,' *widdle, widdle, widdle, 'Aarr!'* that's better and it's got that kid off me. I'll go to bed now and get up tonight for some real fun.

'Yawn,' it's all dark and quiet and I can't see anyone. It must be night, I'll just check, yes it's night alright. Now I'll go and escape . . . but how? I'll try ramming the cage door open, *clang!* Yippee! It's open, now for some fun . . . Oh what's this? It looks big and soft and it's got some big lumpy things on it, I know I'll try climbing up it . . .

Whoa, I'm pooped and I'm hungry, but this thing is very comfy, I think I'll have a rest. *Yum,* look here cake crumbs, *nibble, nibble, nibble.* My favourite. Now it's time to mark some territory, a widdle here, a widdle there, here a widdle, there a widdle, everywhere a widdle.

Now if another hamster comes here I'll give him a shock. I'll shout, 'Oi, no this is my territory!'

'Yawn,' I'm tired, 'Night, night.'

*James Broomhall (11)*
*Beacon Primary School*

# A Day In The Life Of My Cat

Today it's my birthday and I've been up since 4.00 am hoping I get some treats because I'm starving. Quick! I can hear someone coming . .! The door's now opening. It's the small boy . . . Maybe he's come down to give me my birthday treats . . . How disappointing, he only wants a glass of water and now he's going back to bed.

*Five hours later*

Finally I've got my treats and they are delicious. My owners have gone out now so I can run in and out of my cat flap and catch as many birds as possible.

I'm now in the garden and it's my big chance, there's a big bird in the centre of the lawn . . . It's seen me, drat, it's flown up a tree, I will have to chase it.

*Ten minutes later*

I'm stuck up a stupid tree with no bird, thirsty and uncomfortable and it's about two hours before I'm rescued.

*Two hours later*

Finally I am being rescued by the big lady and I think it's the worst day of my life. Ouch, my leg's stuck and the big lady's still pulling me. The pain's getting worse and it's shooting up my back. After a few more tugs I'm finally free. But wait, where is she taking me? No not back inside please. She's putting me down in my basket with that silly blanket that always itches me, but I do have to say I am glad to be back inside and I think that is the last time I will try to catch a bird.

***Jade Evans (11)***
***Beacon Primary School***

# A Day In The Life Of A Clock

I am a clock, an everyday object especially in schools.

Today is Monday, and I can hear the thudding of the teachers stomping their feet on the ground. This means the children will soon be here.

The shouting and screaming is getting louder and louder and the children have just come back from break and are running around the classroom. Good, the teacher is telling them off, peace and quiet at last. They are getting down to some hard work now.

As the teacher warns off one side of the classroom the other children are whispering to each other.

I think the teacher is writing something on the board, and the children are watching her. She might be writing some sums or a piece of writing to copy or worst of all names to miss play.

The teacher has called a name. She could be in trouble. 'Phew she's only the tuck monitor. For a second there I thought she would have been in big trouble.

Yes, it's dinner time, well for 25 minutes. Oh dear, looks like she's writing names on the board. There's Daniel, Peter and Alice and they're getting told off.

Ow! Those bells hurt my ears really badly but they warn me that the children are coming as well.

The children are just finishing off some work and are getting ready for home. I'll be glad when they've gone home. Well until tomorrow anyway.

*K'Lee Green (11)*
***Beacon Primary School***

# A Day In The Life Of A Donkey

It is a bright hot day, all I can wish for is that nobody wants to ride on my back, for I am an old donkey with a black shabby mane. I am at this moment in time, on a hot sandy beach. It's more or less quiet, apart from those loud-mouthed seagulls and apart from the children. Every day they kick their sharp heels into my ribs and they still don't have any feelings for poor donkeys. The children are usually short and tubby.

Oh, what's this, here's a little boy now . . . tall and skinny, makes a change. As he heavily climbs on to my back I begin to slowly walk down the side of the beach. Now I've stopped and the boy has jumped off. My legs feel weak and I fall to the ground. My master is kicking me until I get up - boy can I feel the pain.

The day has passed and now I want some oats or carrots. What is this, barely a handful of sweetcorn! Excuse me whilst I eat this rubbish . . . *chomp! chomp!*

I am fully out of breath, I'm getting too old for this, I am slowly padding along into the tow-truck, it's made of an old jagged box. There's absolutely no room at all, hardly any hay to lie down on and not a drop of water. I have just arrived at the stables where I sleep. The people here treat me a lot better. *Mmmmm,* look at all these oats and all that water.

I'll see you next time. I'm going to tuck in!

*Daniel Orton (9)*
*Birchills CE Primary Community School*

# A Day In The Life Of Henry VIII

Oh today was just so invigorating, the swipe of an axe, the scream of a woman - perfect, just perfect! As you might have guessed it was my old wife Anne's execution today. Lousy woman couldn't even give me a son. Well I suppose I'm being a bit generous, she wasn't good at anything really. She always made me lumpy custard (remind me next time to get a cook instead of a wife).

The execution was very satisfying although it took a long time for the guards to get her down from the tower, what with her kicking and screaming and Princess Elizabeth hanging on to her legs. You should have heard the racket Elizabeth was making. I mean, imagine her being the Queen of England.

The actual execution was short and sweet, the axe went clean through and the head went thud into the basket. To celebrate the success we had a brilliant feast and my favourite roast boar caught by the one and only me! We laughed, we drank, we ate and we danced to my newly composed piece 'Greensleeves'.

Oh yes, and I almost forget to mention, I met another wonderful woman today - her name's Jane Seymour. Maybe I'll have better luck this time.

*Hannah Train (11)*
*Dorridge Junior School*

# A Day In The Life Of An Ant

I've always had a fear of humans. How would you like it if you lived in constant fear of being trodden on by a giant foot, or for that matter, being sprinkled on by ant powder. If you ask me, being an ant is hard, incredibly hard.

I may be little but I'm very strong. I can hold a thousand times my weight. Impressive hey! You have to be hard-working to be a worker ant. Picking up rubbish that may be useful for the nest. Food, however is never a problem. Egg sandwiches, crusts, Walkers crisps, cake crumbs and chips smothered in vinegar are all-time favourites. After lunch we all get back to work and I was scurrying down the road when *thump* . . . a large shoe come crashing down on me. Don't worry, that's only a minor earthquake. If humans are scared of real earthquakes imagine how scared ants are! Problem after problem, next it rained. I went into a house and yes, you guessed it, was thrown out of the window but not the first storey, the third. After free-falling nine metres everything went black. When I awoke I stumbled back to the nest and collapsed in a heap ready for a good forty winks. Well, that's just 'c'est la vie' for an ant!

*Katie Purser (11)*
*Dorridge Junior School*

# A Day In The Life Of A Butterfly

I am here, I made it without being eaten or squashed. It is my first and last day. I will take you through it. At the moment my wings are just drying out.

It is ten minutes later and they're only just dry. I am glad I am out of my chrysalis.

Wow! I am flying for the first time in my whole life, not that I live very long, but this is really good. If I fly high enough I might bump into a bird. Wow! I can see everything from up here, it is brilliant! There is the bush I was laid on and grew up on.

I am going down to a flower but this time I do not have to munch on the chewy leaves. I can suck on the sweet nectar of the lovely perfumed flower with its great coloured petals, they drew me to it. It is a lovely life being a butterfly. I wish I could live a longer life than this. I am going to move on to the next flower. I think I will choose a red flower. Oh but I know the pink ones are lovely. Oh the sweet lovely nectar. I wish I could have sucked on lots of flowers every day when I was a caterpillar.

Let's go, oh no . . .! There is a blue tit after me. Help . . .! If I go down to the plant I can hide in it. He can't get me. He's got me *oouucchh . . !*

*Abigail Waters (11)*
*Dorridge Junior School*

## A Day In The Life Of A Cat

'Yawn!' I had a great hunt last night. I met up with the street's lads and I caught four spiders, a mouse, and a whole (wait for it . . .) rabbit! *'Aaargh'* Oh there's the mistress screaming, she's obviously found the present I left on the doorstep. You should have seen her face when I came in with a live mouse. She'll be off to wake the girls now, if she forgets they'll be late for school and they wouldn't want that! *Thump! Thump! Thump!* Now she's coming to feed me, not that I need it after that succulent mouse. She'll be expecting me to rub around her legs, so I'd better.

*Miaow mmmm! Duck!* My favourite, but I'm not hungry. Oooh! I'm getting the special treatment, a sprinkle of crunchy treats as well. But, but it's being taken away from me. *Noooo!* Phew! It's back but this time full with sparkling clear water. *Slurp!* Deeply refreshing! Any moment now the master will come downstairs and I will hear his footsteps head towards the door. *Aaah*! Here they come, and *whoosh!* I am out, I run with the fresh air blowing my fur in every direction. With every move I feel the earth, leaves and bark are watching me. *Yum!* I have just spotted a butterfly and I fancy a small snack. I'm crawling through the undergrowth, stalking my prey and I *pounce!* I've caught it, I've caught it! *Ooh!* very soft and fluttery in my tummy. Tired and weary I slink back into my territory and fall into a deep sleep.

*Jennifer Hall (11)*
*Dorridge Junior School*

# A Day In The Life Of A Snail

It's so hard being a snail, everything takes so long to do. We don't really use that human term of day and night in the land of snails. But we sometimes creep inside our shells for protection from those swooping living creatures or a human's foot. Us snails never know when something is going to destroy our habitat, or worse, us! Today I have already had a narrow escape from a deadly boot kind of thing, that just missed me by an inch. I suppose us snails are used to it though. We never know when we might close our eyes forever.

Right now I have just been caught in those tight, gripping talons, that have lifted me off the ground. Thud! I have just been dropped, my wounded body aching, as I slowly crawl along trying desperately to find some food to eat. I go into a back garden belonging to a lonely old man. He is very gentle with his sweet scented flowers. I should know as I hid under the leaves of a flower. He doesn't pick me up and throw me down as I eat the leaves of his plants.

My advice is to find the quiet places to loiter or you won't last long in the real world!

*Laura Baker (11)*
*Dorridge Junior School*

# A Day In The Life Of Lara Croft

Today I risked my life fighting and defeating the two killer dogs Boris and Spartakus. I was searching through the woods, being chased by the baddies and I found a machine gun, which soon finished them off.

I then climbed into my speedboat, cruised down the river towards a villa. I entered the code and walked in. Inside it was dark and gloomy. There were pistols lying on the floor and a key was on the table, it was gold and shiny. I picked it up and put it in my rucksack. I climbed up the wooden ladder and heard footsteps. The room was collecting dust and cobwebs hung from the ceiling.

When I reached the top, no one was there. I smashed the window and I could see a man escaping. I fired my gun but I couldn't quite aim straight. He shot back. I dived into the river holding my breath hoping he would go away, but he didn't. I had to come up for air. He saw me and dived in after me. I swam to the speedboat and climbed in and got away.

I looked at my watch. My health monitor was flashing; I didn't have much time to live. When I turned round I realised there was a health pack at the bottom of the river. I dived down with five seconds to grab the pack and get out again.

Would I survive?

*Claire Tolley (11)*
*Dorridge Junior School*

# A Day In The Life Of A Black Immigrant

All my life I wanted my four children to be safe and not to be judged by the colour of their skin but by who they truly are.

A typical day for me would be full of pain and horror inside, some of the words thrown at me, feel like a lifetime of knives stabbing at me. When it gets to midday, when the sun is at its highest it shines on me as if offering sympathy. I must feed my family on what we have. Sometimes I wish that wishes came true and that dreams were really reality.

When I walk out on to the dull London streets to fetch the milk, people shout cruel things. When I try to rub it out, tears trickle down my cheeks because those words will never be erased. With a pinch of hate, a drop of evil, my soul drops lower, reaching the point of my broken heart.

As I climb into bed at night I whisper quietly my prayers, that I may be free. I wonder why my family is looked upon like this. Why should we be judged by the colour of our skin. Please help my soul to rise again and my broken heart fix together, like a jigsaw puzzle. I climb into bed, my eyes close and that fantasy peace life begins.

As a child I looked forward to the future, but now I dread it as I know it brings war - not freedom, I can't swim where I want or smile or laugh. I'm trapped inside this world . . .

*Jennifer Blackhall (11)*
*Dorridge Junior School*

## A Day In The Life Of A Car Sticker

Yippee, yippee, I'm next to be given out I thought, by the way I am a BRMB friendly car sticker. A young man came through the electronic doors at Tesco. I was given to him and he squeezed me tight, it felt like all the life in me had been squeezed out. After going round Tesco I was stuck to the back of the young man's car. I felt stretched, full of life, ready to face the world, and travel it. The car was a brand-new BMW Z3, it even had a private registration number - it was DAV 1D. I looked round and found I was going to live next to a RSPCC sticker. I asked him where he had come from. He said he came from Sainsbury's and he had come to Birmingham from London. Then I asked him where we were going. He didn't know.

*Burr, brum, brum -screech,* these were the sounds that I heard as the car started up. David had turned on the radio now. He was listening to BRMB. I felt pleased. Now we were going down a street, I thought I was travelling the world but apparently this was only Birmingham. The song 'Crazy' by Britney Spears had just finished and the winner of a competition was announced. David started cheering and then he stopped the car and kissed me. I realised that I had made him win lots of money. I felt proud.

*Hayley Wallwork (11)*
*Dorridge Junior School*

# A DAY IN THE LIFE OF AN ORCA WHALE

It was a warm summer's day and the young Orca whale was swimming in the calm, sapphire blue sea. The sky was also blue with not a cloud in sight and the golden sun was about to take its place high in the sky.

The Orca whale lived in a pod consisting of fifteen whales. In the morning they hunted together, searching for fish and other interesting food, grabbing the fish in their jaws. They then leaped and played in front of passing ships, but not all ships were as peaceful as the passenger liners. There were the big fishing ships, with their nylon nets, so strong it was impossible for any creature to escape from one, not even a creature as large as a whale.

When a whale got trapped in a net, the rest of the pod swam over near the unfortunate whale, squeaking unhappily in their little secret language. They then swam near a research ship, leaping unhappily. A scientist on board sensed something was wrong and dived into the water to investigate. He spotted the trapped whale and carefully untangled it.

As well as hunting, playing and a whale getting trapped in a net, the whales met another pod. They examined each other carefully, testing each other to see if they were worth being friendly with.

At the end of the day the whales lounged about in the water, resting after their exciting day.

*Elizabeth Pratt (11)*
*Dorridge Junior School*

# A DAY IN THE LIFE OF BILL GATES

I stepped out of my chauffeur-driven limousine in Silicon Valley in California. I saw the Windows' flags rustling in the wind on the way into the office. I walked into the office and on the desk was the New York Times. On the front page was a picture of Larry Ellison, a competitor of mine. I thought it's good that someone else is on the front page!

On the way to my office I saw my old Uni chum, Steve Ballmer. I said, 'Hi.' I walked on a bit thinking about the three billion dollar deal I was about to complete. I started sweating. I smartened myself up and walked into the meeting. Michael Dell opened his briefcase and pulled out his notes. But then my phone rang, so I answered it. It was Judge Reno about the court case of breaking up my Microsoft empire.
She said, 'I'm not holding back the case any longer, it has to be on Tuesday, or you'll get fined three million dollars.'

I said sorry to Michael Dell but he didn't seem to mind. So we started the negotiations.

We were nearly there, he was about to give me the cheque but then again my phone rang. I answered it, it was Melinda my wife. She wanted me to pick up the kids on the way home. I said to her, 'I should be working out at the gym, I'm getting old now, I'm 45 years old.'

Michael Dell handed me the cheque. I thought *Yes!* Michael Dell left the room. I thought to myself another three billion dollars safely in the bank.

*James Bowser (10)*
*Eversfield Preparatory School*

# A Day In The Life Of David Coulthard

I woke up in my luxurious hotel room. I got changed and walked downstairs to get my breakfast. After breakfast I went to practise for the race this afternoon. I did twenty laps and then I went for a rest thinking about the race. Then my team moved the car into the starting position. I was very apprehensive, my tummy was churning as if elephants were stampeding and I felt a little sick.

At the beginning of the race I was a little nervous. I was hoping it was going to be a great race and we were off. Blasting power pushed the cars forward. I went zooming round the corner.

Twenty laps later I was coming third after a rapid opening to the race and then Schumacher went spinning off the track. I was coming second. Then I wondered if I could possibly win.

Thirty-nine laps later I was still coming second. I was speeding around the track. It was the last lap. I could see the finish line and it was a draw! We needed a replay, then the officials decided, 'It is Coulthard!' I celebrated and went back to my apartment and rested and that was the end of my day.

*William Chamberlain (10)*
*Eversfield Preparatory School*

# A DAY IN THE LIFE OF TIGER WOODS

Tiger started golf at a very young age. Tiger is a very famous golfer. He is very strong and muscular. Tiger won the 1997 Masters and won the Green Jacket and a house. He is twenty-one years old. I spent a day with him talking about gold and more. Tiger is my favourite golfer.

Among the honours received, Woods was chosen by The Associated Press as the male athlete of the year for the second time in three years. He became only the seventh man and the second golfer to earn the award twice since it began in 1931. The others were Byron Nelson, Don Budge, Sandy Koufax, Carl Lewis, Joe Montana and Michael Jordan who won three times. Woods' career earnings to date are $14,641,832 including $11,837,129 on the PGA tour. His 750 points earned in 1999 were also a record. In the 1997 Masters, Woods had a record score of 270, 18 under par at Augusta National Golf Club, and won by a record margin of twelve strokes. Tiger at age two was putting with Bob Hope. For nine holes he shot 48 at age three.

*Sam Jamison (10)*
*Eversfield Preparatory School*

## A Day In The Life Of The Loch Ness Monster

*'Ahh.* What is that loud noise?' I grumbled.
I rose from the water and I could see a huge man playing the bagpipes.
*'Shh!'* I shouted at the man.
He suddenly ran off screaming and shouting, *'Ha, ha!.'*
'What a wimp,' I said. 'I feel very hungry, what shall I have?'

Suddenly a huge school of fish zoomed by the side of me. 'I think I will get my breakfast from them.' I started swimming towards them. I was about to grab the whole school when suddenly a huge block fell into the water.

'Wow!' I cried. The block had fallen from an old castle overlooking Loch Ness. 'I'm going to the surface to see what's happening.' I arrived at the surface and saw a news reporter on the shore. I could not hear the news reporter, so I went closer.

I then could hear the news reporter's voice, she was saying, 'Loch Ness is the longest lake in Scotland, home to the legend Nessie. This lake is very important because very old castles overlook it. Kirsty Young, reporting for the Ten O'clock News,' she concluded.

'It's time I should go to bed for a few more hundred years. Goodbye,' I concluded.

*Oliver Lowson (10)*
*Eversfield Preparatory School*

## A DAY IN THE LIFE OF MR MOORCROFT

I woke up in the morning and went to open the factory doors to Moorcroft Pottery, my factory. When I got there I opened the doors. I went to the office, I put down my briefcase and sat at my desk. I saw an envelope on my desk top addressed to me so I opened it and found that Mr Smith had written to me to ask my factory to make a pot with a picture of a man doing work on it.

I ran into the glazing part of the factory and told them what Mr Smith wanted and everyone said that they would be delighted to make this design. I rushed into the pot making part of the factory and asked them to make a large fattish pot with a handle to contain water.

Then I went back into my office and opened my diary to see what else was happening today. I found that a tour was booked for two o'clock which was in five minutes. I dashed as fast as I could through all the parts of the factory, warning everybody and then I dashed again to the door just in time to see them come in. I said, 'Welcome to Moorcroft, I hope you enjoy your tour around the factory.'

After the tour I said 'Goodbye,' and off they went.

*Elliot Mintz (10)*
*Eversfield Preparatory School*

# A Day In The Life Of Prince William

I woke up at 8.30am definitely not looking forward to another horrible day of 'A' level exams at Eton College, London. That night I had slept happily at the boarding part of the school, so all that I had to do was to go and collect my friend, Helen and go down to breakfast with her.

After I was ready for the school day I said, 'Goodbye' to Helen and walked back upstairs to the bedrooms where I opened the curtains and then immediately closed them again because there were millions of photographers outside, so I calmly went to the first exam room.

The master kindly welcomed me in the usual, special, respectful way. I sat down at the front desk but by now there were photographers everywhere that I looked, so the exam master, very frustrated, shooed them away.

The other morning exams proceeded in the same boring fashion, and when it was time for delicious lunch I was extremely relieved that I was completely free from photographers. I was quite disappointed when lunch finished but I knew that I had to carry on with exams. I would have rather been eating chicken casserole than writing about experiments in chemistry!

The afternoon exams were as hectic as the morning ones so when the school day had ended I felt like letting out a big scream! I rapidly calmed myself down and changed into some suitable clothes for a hopefully relaxing evening.

*Matthew Simpson (10)*
*Eversfield Preparatory School*

# A Day In The Life Of David Beckham

I got in my Ferrari, strapped Brooklyn in and went down to Wembley. After I had got changed I jogged on to the pitch to practice. The crowd were cheering loudly.

I got the ball and passed it to Alan Shearer who crossed it. I headed it in the back of the net. At half-time we were 2-0 up. Kevin Keegan talked to us. We went back on the pitch. Alan Shearer passed it to me. I ran and got fouled. I stepped up and blasted the ball into the back of the net! We were 3-0 up and Kevin started to make some changes. He substituted G Neville for Southgate. And then something amazing happened, Portugal came up and scored and then we were suddenly 3-3. It went into penalties. I scored and we won. I went home, got in my jacuzzi and then went to bed.

*Ben Taylor (10)*
*Eversfield Preparatory School*

# A Day In The Life Of Michael Owen

I woke up at 6.30am and I thought I must get up for training. I had had an almost sleepless night thinking about the big Euro 2000 game ahead of England. We were playing Germany.

I went to training and everybody was already there. We started to do a practice match. After that Kevin Keegan showed us the team tactics for tonight.

After the practice match we rushed to the leisure centre and ran to the gym. Funnily enough I didn't feel remotely nervous. After about forty-five minutes of training in the gym, the team cooled off in the swimming pool and some went in the jacuzzi.

After that I drove home to think about what I was going to do during the match. Three hours after that I drove in my blue BMW to Wembley. After I had got changed and warmed up England walked onto the pitch. I heard some words of abuse from the German fans. I felt angry but didn't say anything.

After half-time it was still 0-0. At full-time we had won 1-0 after an excellent cross from David Beckham and a header from Alan Shearer.

Because Kevin Keegan was so pleased with us we got a bonus in our pay. We also spent the entire night in the pub.

*Edmund Westlake (10)*
*Eversfield Preparatory School*

## A DAY IN THE LIFE OF DAVID BECKHAM

In the morning I woke up at 3.30am and started going out for my early morning jog. Brooklyn was crying, then Victoria started to sing but that only made it worse!

Then, when I finally went out for my early morning jog, I saw Michael Owen on the pitch, injured. I rang up Kevin Keegan and I said, 'Owen's out for the game.'
He said 'Blast!'
Then I rang up Victoria and said, 'Bring some bandages to Owen's house.'
Michael said, 'Here is my house key, take me inside.'
Then a knock at the door came, it was Victoria with the bandages. We left the bandages and went.

Then in my Ferrari I sped to the training ground and when I parked I saw Gareth Southgate. He told me that Reebok had sponsored him. I said, 'I am pleased for you.'

In training there were a lot of fouls so I took lots of free kicks for practice.

After, I went to the bank and took £500 and then I said, 'I hope Nicky Clarke will give me change this time!'

*Simon Barley (10)*
*Eversfield Preparatory School*

# A Day In The Life Of Alan Shearer

At eight o'clock in the morning Alan Shearer got up early for training. 'Oooaaahhh! let's get goin' for the big game today!'

When he got dressed he sped in his S-type Jaguar to the stadium to play Germany on Saturday.

Once he arrived at the stadium he met Kevin Keegan.
'Hi Kev,' said Shearer.
'Hi ya Al,' replied Kevin Keegan.
They started training from 10.00am to 12.20pm.
'Hey Kev, I'm a bit parched, can I get a drink?' said Shearer.

After training, Shearer went to his private hotel not far away to rest for six hours.

Now it was 6.30pm, one hour before the match, and Shearer went back to the stadium to train for half an hour while the crowd were there.

Fifteen minutes before kick-off there was a team talk.
'Alright lads, this is a big game coming up, and millions of viewers are watching. Let the ball do the work, be skilful, enthusiastic, and aggressive. Now go out there and show me some football, *right*!'

After the match they received £15,000,000 and knew that their work was not finished yet.

*David Cross (10)*
*Eversfield Preparatory School*

# A Day In The Life Of Mike Atherton

Mike Atherton will get up in the morning and go straight to training. At training he practices his batting and fielding and bowling with his left hand. He trains much harder on match days. He goes home for an hour or so after going to the pavilion for a drink.

When he goes home for a few hours before his match at 8 o'clock, he goes back at 6 o'clock for one hours training before the match.

Half an hour before the match against the West Indies and just before he walks out to the field to bat, the nerves rise. Before the match, Mike Atherton and Nasser Hussain flipped a coin to see who would face the first ball. Mike lost the toss and ended up facing the first ball with Walsh bowling. The umpire said, 'Start the match.' He put his hand behind his back and Walsh started to make his run up. The ball went flying straight to Mike Atherton. Atherton hit the ball and it went for four. On the second ball the wicket keeper missed the ball and it went for four.

Then Walsh got him out for LBW, he walked off calmly to the pavilion, took his pads off and said 'That was never out!' Next he went to the pavilion to watch the rest of the match. England's batsmen went in to bat one by one and the most runs scored were thirty. England were all out for 179 runs. 'It's time for tea' the umpire said just as England's last batsman went out. There was half an hour for tea and then the West Indies got padded up for their innings.

When Mike goes out he wants to get Walsh out so he bowled and he got Walsh out and he also caught three other people but sadly they lost by two runs. When the match had finished he went home and went and had a shower.

*Joe White (10)*
*Eversfield Preparatory School*

## A Day In The Life Of Victor The Earthworm

Slowly I circled Maliday, ready to strike, to kill, to win. My hour of glory had come! Victory! Power! Death!

'Victor!' A loud and vibrant voice awoke me. I groaned. Yet again, just a dream.

Laboriously, I got out of bed and washed. Then, feeling a little peckish, I had some earthflakes for breakfast. I didn't eat much before I discovered that I was very, very late! At once I grabbed my trowel and rushed off to school.

I was greeted at school by Mrs Wormwood, my teacher. She complained coldly that I was late, before continuing with her lesson on the art of ornamental digging. I sat back and yawned. This was going to be dull.

Lunchtime - yuck! Weed sandwiches *again*. And mud crisps are terrible (too sour for my taste). Of course, it would be butterfly cakes with soil chips - just to complete my ghastly lunch!

I decided that I needed some foul air, so I left my lunch and climbed up the nearest shaft. I came out in a *jungle* of grass and moss, and after just a little exploration I was quite lost!

Suddenly, I felt the grass shaking. A caterpillar rushed past me. It seemed very frightened. I didn't run. I'm glad I didn't. If I had, that huge, human boy wouldn't have put me in a box and taken me metres away to his home. And I wouldn't be here now, eating trifle and herbs - not going to school.

Now I have told you the story, bye! I need my beauty sleep.

*Isabel Richards (10)*
*Four Oaks Junior School*

# A Day In The Life Of The Jabberwocky

I woke up and stretched my claw-like toes, and scratched my scaly skin, ready for my great fight with Prince Phillip. As I readied my wings for a flight a giant herd of dust came hurtling towards me, and it sent me flying backwards. As I fell to the ground I heard, 'Beware my son, beware my son of the Jabberwocky, the jaws that bite, the claws that snatch.' I remembered that I am the Jabberwocky, I got up and began flying and gliding when I stopped to see the king and his son, the great Prince Phillip, who has slain every last monster except me and my great dangerous friends, the Jub Jub Bird and Shun the Bandesnatch.

Look at him, standing there with his fancy sword, thinks he can slay me. He hasn't fought in a long time so he can't slay me. He's sitting by the Tum Tum trying to make a plan, if he comes near me I'll crush him like a can.

I finally made my move, I was burbling as I went through a lucky wood. I flapped my wings and sent him flying back, *smack!* I went galloping back, I tried to dodge, oh how I tried to dodge but that young prince was too fast, as he flashed and slashed. The pain, he'd slain me and hung my head on his wall.

*James Hughes (10)*
*Four Oaks Junior School*

# A Day In The Life Of Homer J Simpson

There I was minding my own business when suddenly the door smashed open. A group of motorbikes called 'The Hell Satans' tried to kill me. I made a deal that if they didn't kill me they could hang around my house.

After work I walked in and my house, what a dump. It was as messy as a pig sty but everyone was gone. Later that day we realised something was missing. After a lot of thought Bart said, 'Dad there's a note on your head.'
So I took it off my head and read it. It said, 'Thanks for letting us hang out, by the way we took your wife.'
'Doh' I replied.

So I drove to a bar called the 'Slaughter House' and asked it they'd seen my wife, they chucked me out. I found my wife and started to attack. He grabbed a chain and started to hit me.
'Oo, ahh, ow, stop it,' I yelled.
We walked into the 'ring of death' and started a duel with motorbikes. I dropped my motorbike but my wife threw it back. I had him cornered. I was just about to hit him but he said 'Nooo, have her back, I give up.' Then I drove back to the 'Slaughter House', walked in and stole some Duff beer.

*Billy McGrail (10)*
*Four Oaks Junior School*

## A Day In The Life Of A Caterpillar

Just another day, eating my usual leaf for breakfast. Mmm, fresh from the bush. Soon I will be the most beautiful butterfly, I told myself. As soon as I have finished my breakfast I'm going back to sleep. When I finished I went straight to bed and I started to dream. Suddenly I was awoken by a very loud bang. It was a giant (actually a person). 'Aaarrhh!' I screamed. I dodged his foot as he trod on my house. I ran as quickly as I could, trying to reach my friend's house.

As soon as I reached her house I told her about what happened and she said I could stay there. I was shivering like mad as I thought about it, going near to death. My friend Katy brought me some hot chocolate and a leaf to calm me down. She told me to rest but I couldn't. I decided to collect some leaves for my friend to thank her for letting me stay. But as soon as I left the house I saw another giant. This time he was behind me so I couldn't go to the house, I was too afraid. I quickly spun a cocoon and jumped in, I knew he couldn't get me now.

*Daniel Longmore (10)*
*Four Oaks Junior School*

# A Day in The Life Of A Slug

As I got up from my usual snooze I stretched my body. My log was damp and moist, just as I had left it the night before. I slithered out of the brown, flaky log and down the path, as I usually do. I was slithering down the path looking for a nice, tasty, green leaf for my breakfast. Then I heard a thud, thud, thud and then I saw a heavy foot stamp two inches away from my head. Well, I thought that was the end of me but it wasn't. Then I saw another huge foot thunder down in front of me. I slithered into the soil and started to nibble at Mrs Robinson's cabbage patch. Then out came Peter the gardener. He came up to the cabbage patch and sprinkled slug pellet all over the plants. 'Ah!' Time to hide I thought so I scampered out of the way.

After Peter had gone I went back to the patch where I was before and I started nibbling again. I suddenly saw a blue shimmering pellet and I thought to myself, 'Hmm, tasty.' So I slithered over to it and then I couldn't remember the last thing that happened to me.

*Sam Parsons (10)*
*Four Oaks Junior School*

# A Day In The Life Of A Penguin

Why, oh why, oh why do I have to be a penguin? It's not fair. Today I've woken up to the horrible cold winter snow with my chick on my feet. She's moaning because she has not had her breakfast. I waddled up to the sea to catch some food. Soon I'll huddle with the rest. How I wish to go on holiday. What was that? A rumble?

'Aahhh!' I screamed.
'Your wish is my command,' a voice boomed.
Suddenly it happened, the chick jumped off my feet and . . .
'I'm in the air, it feels great, I'm going as fast as a sports car on a road with no traffic.' I'm crying excitedly wondering where I was going to end up.

As soon as I landed I looked around, up, down, to the left, to the right, everywhere, it was amazing. The sun shone as bright as polished metal. A cock also screeched happily whilst sunbathing, the sand under my feet twinkled like stars.

I decided to make my first move. First of all I went to the beach cafe for a nice, cool ice-lolly, then to the beach for a sunbathe. I went to sleep for ages, then woke up, I was homesick so I wished to go back as fast as I could. I spinned home. When I got back everyone was looking for me.

*Emily Jackson (9)*
*Four Oaks Junior School*

# A Day In The Life Of A Turtle

I woke up from my soft bed (a bundle of leaves) with my shell polished from the previous rainfall. I lifted my cramped fin and swept some water from my eyes which were full of sand. I stretched my hind legs and stood up and slowly plodded along trying to find a breakfast. I could see nothing apart from some leaves that were dead, and were rotting like mad. I searched some more until I came to a big bundle of luscious leaves, I couldn't resist. I mean I hadn't eaten in days. I started to tuck in.

I hadn't eaten in days because I had been so busy. I hadn't seen such a beautiful sight in ages. The leaves were glittering under a sunbeam that was peeking through branches on the trees.

I was as happy as a fox full of food. I decided to take a nap. I was too tired anyway, five miles is enough for one morning.

I woke up tired and couldn't be bothered to do anything. I lifted my armoured shell which was still polished from the previous rainfall. I kept plodding along trying to find a lake to drink from that would sparkle off the sun's rays. I kept plodding along as far as my legs would take me.

I started to become disappointed, but then I saw a glittering, space-like river. I drank some, it was as fresh as ever. I then found out it was near teatime.

I came back to my bed, I was too tired to eat so I just lay down and went to sleep knowing that I had a lovely day.

*Robert Stainforth (10)*
*Four Oaks Junior School*

# A Day In The Life Of A Rabbit

One cloudy day two children went to a pet shop. They bought two rabbits, Blacky and Poppy. Poppy had four baby rabbits, then eight and so on till she had sixteen. The rabbits were too much for them to look after, so they kept one and got rid of all the rest.

A couple of years later I had grown up and we decided to move house. We got to the last day, my mum went to feed him and he got out. Next to us was a park, we never saw the rabbit again.

Now we have moved we have got a guinea pig called Smoky, another rabbit called Blacky Two. My aunt has got two guinea pigs. They are called Nutmeg and Liquorice. One is black and one is ginger. She has also got two dogs, Tiger and Kimmie. Kimmie is black and Tiger is the same as a tiger. They did have a rabbit which was six weeks old. A couple of days later he died. My rabbit escaped from his hutch into the park. He sometimes comes back to see me. I go to the park and see him on Saturdays.

*Samantha Hough (10)*
*Four Oaks Junior School*

# A Day In The Life Of Codder And Stan

Hello! I am Codder, I have a faithful pet, Stan. We travel through the cod world, Stan electrocuting plaice and rainbow trout on the way. I am a magician fish (magifish for short) and I am famous all over the cod world.

This is different. Here's how it started. I was in my office when I heard:
'Stan to Codder! Stan to Codder!'
I said, 'OK.'
I swam to Stan's office rather reluctantly because I was in the middle of planning my next act.
'What is it?'
Stan said, 'It's your boss.'
'What about him?' I said worriedly.
'He's ill,' Stan said.
'Get lost Stan,' I shouted, blowing Stan into the wall. 'What has he ever done to me?'
'Er!' Stan squeaked.
'No!' I shouted 'So I shouldn't help him!'
And I swam out fast and slammed the door.

I stayed in my office for four short hours when again I heard:
'Stan to (sniff) Codder. Stan (sniff) to (sniff) Codder.'
There was a silence then . . .
'What now?' I bawled down the microphone. All I heard was a (sniff, sniff) through the phone.

After that I was barking mad at Stan for saying what he said to me. I was so mad, infact I smashed the line from my phone to Stan's office.

Hours later a spark hit my desk. A phone call from Stan. More sparks started to fly and a barrage of sparks flew at me. They hit me. Then I heard:
'Serves you right if these sparks hit you . . .'

*Samuel Hepburn (10)*
*Four Oaks Junior School*

## A DAY IN THE LIFE OF ARNOLD SCHWARZENEGGER

'My name is Arnold Schwarzenegger, I'm a very famous actor.' I stormed into the TV studios feeling very grumpy.
'Hey Arnie what's the matter' called the editor.
'Oh shut up' boomed Sylvester Stallone. 'What's up? You look really down in the dumps today, man,' he said again.
'It's getting up too early, that's what it is,' I complained.
'When are we going to start filming anyway?'
'Now,' said the weenie producer.
'Come on then, I want to go home early tonight because my wife is coming home from Norway.'

Later that day during the film making -
'Get down.'
*Bang, bang, bang,* the noise from the bullets hitting the car.
'Cut! That was good but . . .'
'What. What was wrong with that, hey?' I screamed.
'You have to get your aim better.'
*'I don't care I just want to go home today, well at least sometime today anyway.'*
'OK, you want to see your wife, but we have to finish this film today.'

A good while later:
'James, I'm going to miss you, but I hope this will make you remember me.'
*Splash* as he threw the dead body into the river.
'Brilliant,' shouted the producer, just brilliant.
'I'm going home now!'
'But we need t . . .'
Slam came the sound of the door.

*Liam Woods (10)*
*Four Oaks Junior School*

## A Day In The Life Of Dennis Bergkamp

As we walked out on to the pitch I felt very nervous. I was representing the Dutch team as captain. I lined up on the pitch and shook hands with the French captain, Zinedine Zidane. I won the toss and chose to kick-off. My team-mate, Patrik Kliuvert, passed the ball to me and I started to dribble with it. I dummied Henry and passed it to Ronald de Boer. He took a shot but Fabien Barthez brilliantly saved it and it went out for a corner. Overmars took the corner quickly. I jumped and headed the ball into the goal!

'And it's a goal! Bergkamp has done it again!'
'We're leading!' shouted Overmars.
We had only played ten minutes of the match. We were playing France.

I called for the ball in the twentieth minute. Seedorf passed it to me but Djorkaeff tackled me. He ran off with the ball and lobbed it to Zidane but De Boer pushed him over!
'Penalty!'
I looked at him in despair. Desailly came up to take it. He kicked the ball and Westerveld saved it!
'Great save by the keeper!'
The referee blew the whistle for half-time and we walked off, leading by 1-0.
'Right then Dennis' said my coach, 'You are coming off for Frank De Boer.' That was the end of my game ...

At the end of the match we received our awards.
'Yeahh!'

*Adam Moore (10)*
*Four Oaks Junior School*

## A Day In The Life Of A Seal

A typical boring day to wake up to in the morning. My fellow seals making a wake-up call. So now it's food time! You've got to be careful in these parts to fish with great white sharks hunting you. Seals like me are a good meal. We seals are all the same, cockled grey skin, eyes as shiny as well polished shoes, white whiskers and teeth as sharp as needles. In the water we can glide through the sea like knives going through the air.

Now for a long important swim to the best fishing ground for a good meal that will last us for the whole winter. One problem, to complete the journey there is a barrier of messy and muddy litter that can do fatal damage to our blubber. If that happens we descend to the arctic depths of the ocean. Most of us will get through easily but some can get mortal wounds. I wish people wouldn't dump all this waste in the sea because you see there's tonnes of oil on the surface which makes it impossible for us to breathe which is the main reason for us dying.

If we finally make it there will be a nesting ground for us to have a little rest after holding our breath for so long. After about an hour we've got to catch some fish so our mates and us won't starve.

When we get home I wonder what tomorrow will bring us.

*Chris Cutler (10)*
*Four Oaks Junior School*

# A Day In The Life Of Geri Halliwell

Hi, my name is Geri Halliwell, I have a very busy life. My day is very busy to begin with and it carries on throughout the day. First of all I get up, and get some breakfast, watch some television and go up the stairs to get dressed.

It's usually a big rush to get into the studios because of all the press will do anything to see you, it does get annoying. So I usually get to the studios abut 9.30am, then the work begins.

I start to begin to record my next song, it's a secret what the title will be, so I won't tell you. Recording is really hard because you have to get everything just right. I usually do that until about 12 o'clock, where you get a break for about an hour and a half. What I do during my lunch break is to go to the canteen, it's very formal but everyone is really nice. I have my lunch, then I drink an awful lot of water because singing for a whole morning doesn't do an awful lot of good for your throat.

Then I go back to do the session in the afternoon and go home and have a shower. Do a bit of paperwork (which I hate), order a pizza, then go to bed.

*Seth Taylor (10)*
*Four Oaks Junior School*

## A Day In The Life Of A Cat

'Good morning, new day,' I said.
The tree at the back of the garden was swaying to and fro in the wind. I got out of my basket, scratched at my scratching post and had a stretch, then I heard my owner come down the stairs and put some food in my bowl. I started to gobble it greedily.

I noticed that my owner was opening the back door to let some air in, so I ran outside into the bushes. It was amazing, there were holes everywhere, some in the fence and some even going underground, my adventure has begun!

I went down one of the holes in the ground. It was dark and gloomy down the hole, the walls were wet and slimy. I didn't like it one bit, I ran up the tube and out into the open air. I didn't really like it down the hole so I decided to stay in the house. So I went back out of the bush and into the house.

Upstairs my master's son was building a model car. I knew he would play with me if I went up but I was too tired to play, so I went to my favourite resting place, and went to sleep.

*James Pope (10)*
*Four Oaks Junior School*

## A Day In The Life Of Miss McKenzie

'Monday mornings, I hate Monday mornings! End of the glorious weekend,' groaned Miss McKenzie. She got out of bed and went downstairs to breakfast. 'Yum, yum,' muttered Miss McKenzie, 'cornflakes and tea!' She had her breakfast and went back upstairs to get dressed.

At about 8 o'cock Miss McKenzie got everything ready for class 5M at school. 'Torture time' thought Miss McKenzie. As the bell rang 5M poured into the classroom. The first lesson was maths, that went by like a whizz. The second lesson was drama, that went by like a whizz too! Infact all the lessons went like a whizz!

Anyway, when home time came I was so relieved. When I got home I just flopped into an armchair and fell asleep!
'Tuesday tomorrow, sleep time for me' thought Miss McKenzie wearily.
'Elaine, time for your dinner!' said Miss McKenzie's mum!

*Charlotte Smith (10)*
*Four Oaks Junior School*

## A Day In The Life Of Grandfather Four Winds

'I am Grandfather Four Winds, grandfather of the Indian Wind tribe. I am the fourth grandfather that's why I am called Four Winds. I am sitting in my spirit field, just imagine the golden sun shining amongst the long green grass and the beautiful pink blossom trees. Shhh, smmm, breathe in and out, and now I must heal the people of this village.'

'My first patient is you Rising Moon, complaining of throat ache, now let's get on . . . there you are Rising Moon, wait a minute I have no one else on my list, the whole of my village is well, we must celebrate! Decorate the village, get your instruments and set up the fire!'

'Just look at how high my warm, blazing, colourful fire is, look at how the stars twinkle, but the mist covering the sky is a sign from my fellow gods to stop the celebration! Put out the fire, take down the decorations!'

'After all the hurrying we are safe, the spirits have protected us, Grandfather Four Winds.'

*Natasha Emmerson (10)*
*Four Oaks Junior School*

# A Day In The Life Of A Knickerbocker Glory Dragon

It was a weird, murky morning and I was staring out of the window to see a colourful sky.

I went in the garden to play after breakfast. My mum died and now I live with my bossy aunt, she is as wicked as a witch. She always goes on about not going to the caves in the woods but I thought to myself why should my aunt boss me about.

So I went to the caves in the mysterious woods and I heard a flutter and I shook with fright. I went closer to this scary noise. My feet shuffled across the ground like a horse's hooves clomping on the floor. I went inside the gloomy cave and there sat on a stony rock looking startled was a dragon. Its multicoloured wings beamed with light outside.

I whispered in a reassuring voice, 'What's your name little one?'
In a timid voice and a squeaky one too he said 'Knickerbocker Glory from the banks of Saint Gloo.' I was left here when I came to collect maple leaves to eat.'
I murmured, 'I will get you home, I'll climb on your back if that's alright?'
He replied 'OK.'

We flew in the air as the breeze whooshed past us. We landed and came to a fantasy land, where noises whined. So I dropped the little, petite dragon with his family. Some dust flew me home to have my supper and then I snuggled down in my cosy bed.

*Rebecca Amyes (10)*
*Four Oaks Junior School*

# A Day In The Life Of Homer Simpson

As I opened my yellow eyes on Sunday morning I heard Marge yell, 'Homer get ready for church, we're going to be late.'
'Alright, I'm coming, I'm coming' I shouted.

I got out my church pants and a hour of TV watching later I was in the car listening to the radio hoping New York would beat Chicago in the basketball game. Today's sermon was about the damage we're causing to the environment, and as usual I fell asleep on the first word he said.

'Homer wake up, sermon's over,' Marge said one hour later.
As soon as I got home I switched on the TV and watched Eye on Springfield.
'A shock defeat for the Chicago Bulls against the New York Lakers. This means that this man is now a billionaire,' reported Kent Brockman.
'Oh I wish I was a billionaire,' I said sadly. 'Hang on,' I said to myself 'that's me!' I screamed 'I'm a billionaire.'
'Homie stop jumping, you're going to jump on the cat,' Marge said.
'But Marge . . .' I started.
'I don't care if you've just become a billionaire that's no excuse for almost killing the cat,' Marge told me.
'But I have just become a billionaire!' I said.
'Hey there neighbour, you hear I've just become a billionaire?' Flanders asked.
'No' I answered, 'I thought I just became a billionaire.'
'They put the wrong picture in front of the camera,' Flanders said.
'Doh!' I yelled.

*Steven Rowley (10)*
*Four Oaks Junior School*

# A Day In The Life Of Tracy Beaker

I was woken up by Cam. Every two minutes she shouted to me 'Are you ready for school?' I finally emerged from the stairs dressed for school but I still hadn't brushed my hair so Cam gave me a brush, I had to sit there for ten minutes brushing my stupid old hair.

I wanted to walk to school on my own but Cam insisted on walking with me and she had to see me inside. I always hated going to school every day. I usually bunk off, but today I was determined to stay all day at school. I took a deep breath and walked into the classroom. I sat down in my place and wrote a letter saying why I hadn't been in the last three days and then I faked Cam's signature. I went up and gave it to my teacher.
'You were sick were you Tracy, are you alright now?'
'Yes' I said.

I sat quietly and waited for the bell for break time. Finally the bell went and it was brilliant to get some fresh air. The whole day went like that and I was always hoping for the hometime bell. Now I am walking home from school but at least I can go home now. I got home and went to my room to read. I lay on my bed and started to read a vampire book when I fell asleep to dream peacefully.

*Rachel Feasey (10)*
*Four Oaks Junior School*

## A Day In The Life Of Neil Armstrong

I woke early that morning, my name is Neil Armstrong and this is the day I visited the moon. As I got dressed I wondered what to expect, would I find something amazing or would something go wrong? I just did not know. When I arrived at NASA there were many photographers surrounding my car. They asked many questions like, 'Do you think the mission will go according to plan?'

I just rushed past them trying to get to the entrance of the massive NASA building. As I walked towards a man holding my spacesuit I stared at it, it sparkled in the light. The man placed the helmet on my head, I felt quite confused, I did not know why.

When my suit was all firmly on and I was in the spacecraft I switched on all the buttons and as if by magic the spacecraft was lit up glamourously, '3, 2, 1, blast-off!'

The spacecraft burst into space with a ball of fire. As I glided through the air the sky started to go darker and after a while we were up in space. The moon was hurtling towards us at quite a high speed.

About half an hour later the door hatch would be ready to be opened. Are you ready? Set . . . go! Pusshh. I jumped out and stepped onto the moon's strange surface and I said, 'One small step for man, one giant step for mankind.'

I returned to the spacecraft knowing the mission was . . . complete!

As I landed back on Earth and opened the hatch I knew my life had been made complete and that was the day I visited the moon.

*Bradley McDowall (10)*
*Four Oaks Junior School*

## HER TIME CAME TOO SOON

One person who inspired me was my Auntie Lisa. We had a long, strong relationship. My Auntie Lisa was an understanding person. She was there for me when there was something stuck in my head like if I was confused.

I could share my untold secrets and she could tell me hers. She was like a gift from God. I felt like she was too good for me.

It all started when my auntie had to take tablets. She was just fine until one day she had a bad reaction and she refused to take tablets.

Then it started. She became ill. She got depressed and she did not know what to do. She did not tell me her secrets anymore and I got worried, I could no longer see her in that state. I was devastated.

Everyone rushed up to the flat when hearing the bad news. It was a surprise to see no Auntie Lisa. We looked in all the rooms but Auntie Lisa wasn't there. When we looked in the bathroom we were shocked to find my Auntie Lisa sitting on the toilet, she was a different colour. It was devastating.

She was a warm and comforting person, she always cared for herself and others. She was always there when people needed her. My very good auntie - Auntie Lisa.

She was my inspiration to be good in everything. She said be happy for what you are.

*Dominique Paisley (9)*
*George Betts Primary School*

## ONE DAY AT A TIME

My nan was a very brave person. My nan didn't tell anyone about her illness. She never cried or got upset, so it became hard for people in her family to cope because she never confided in anyone. This is a little bit about how she inspired me.

My nan was the kind of person that never gave up and was always trying her hardest to be a good grandmother and mother. She often took me out on day trips she was very special to me she understood me for what I am not for what I did. She always told me never to stop trying and that there was light at the end of the tunnel. I never doubted my nan about if she was going to do something she always did it even through the hardest times we always pulled through. My nan was like an angel on my shoulder always looking out for me. That is why I loved her so much. My nan cared a lot about me and brought me gifts nearly every week and that was not why I loved her. It was the love that she showed me.

In the end Jean Blick died and went to heaven she was too good in life to be forgotten. She was my inspiration.

*Syria Ewers (9)*
*George Betts Primary School*

## MY MOTHER

I am inspired by my mum. The way she copes with all of us is amazing. She owns a shop and cares about her children too.

My mum helps me when I have a problem. She has inspired me to be responsible. She has time to cook and wash my hair and comb my hair. When I get low scores for my tests, she encourages me and says I can do well if I try. She helps me when I have a problem or when I am crying.

My gran died seven years ago. She helped me to calm down, she even helped me calm down on my sister's wedding day.

She helps me when I cook, and I forget to put the gas on. When I go on the motorway and I fall asleep, my mum wakes me up when we get to the half-way bridge. She says, 'Wake up Manny!' When it was parents' evening, she said to me 'You've done really good except when you didn't bring your reading book home.' I am inspired by my mother.

*Manjinder Dhesi (10)*
*George Betts Primary School*

## A Day In The Life Of Neil Armstrong

I was flying through space, then the alarm went off. Air was going quickly. They started to make repairs. We were heading for the moon. We were going to crash. We landed with a bang! We were stranded on the moon.

We called NASA, they were sending a spacecraft up straight away. They came and took us towards Earth, then they lost course. We were heading for the dark side of the moon where the fireballs were. We just missed one. Five minutes later we were one mile from Earth. We were in the atmosphere, we had landed and got out.

We were presented with gold medals and we were on live television and we were famous.

*William Reynolds (11)*
*Grove Vale Primary School*

# A Day In The Life Of Y2J

I got out of my bed to see posters of me doing the walls of Jericho on Kurt Angle, then I had my breakfast, brushed my teeth and got in my limo and went to Madison Square Garden.

I found myself in the ring shouting 'Raw is Jericho!' and hitting Gurrero. It was a really big fight but Chyna, Latino Heat. Eddy Gurrero's girlfriend came in after I did the triple power bomb. She tried to hit me with a steel chair. I ducked and I grabbed the chair, smashed it off her head, then pinned Latino Heat and won the European Championship.

The bell went ding, ding! and Chris Benoit, former Intercontinental Champion, who lost from Rikishi on smackdown. He whacked me with some steel steps and did the crippler crossface, until I passed out. Then I was taken on a stretcher to the backstage area. When I woke up I was fine and I heard Chris Roboto's music, so I got out of my room while doctors were screaming at me, 'Don't go, you've got a condition!' I ran out to the Titron and I did the 'walls of Jericho' until the Crippler, Chris Roboto passed out. Then I ran backstage to the parking lot and got in my limo and raced off home.

I got home at 10.00pm and struggled into bed.

*Carl Tinsley (11)*
*Grove Vale Primary School*

## A Day In The Life Of David Coultard

I woke up Sunday morning in Monaco. I was getting ready for a big race. From my hotel room it is a ten minute drive or a fifteen minute run. I chose to run to get to the pits. When I got there, I found where my car was, my F1 McLaren. I found it next to Mika Häkkinen's F1 McLaren.

The pit-men were getting the car ready for the race, putting in the petrol and checking it all over. The time flew by and soon it was time to race. I do a warm-up lap. I was second on the grid Monaco red . . . green - all go on the Monaco Grand Prix.

72 laps to go on the straight. Schumacker first and me second. Häkkinen third, quick turn I'm on the inside, straight round him. It's now me first, Schumacker second and Häkkinen third. On the later stages of the race, Schumacker's engine blew up, so he was out of the race but Schumacker's team mate is third.

The race time ticked away, and it was soon the end.

I came first 'Yes!' I am only 12 points behind Schumacker.

This is the bit I love, soaking people with champagne, my trophy is the biggest trophy, so then they gave me the champagne and of course everyone got wet. My girlfriend was so pleased and I was so pleased with myself.

That's my day in the life of David Coultard - I wouldn't swap lives, not ever.

*Adam Dodd (11)*
*Grove Vale Primary School*

# A Day In The Life Of Fabien Barthez

Last month on a sunny day, I woke up at 8:00 and had a full French breakfast. At 9:00 I drove to the French training ground. The French team were in training for the biggest match in our history against Brazil. We finished training and the French team went to a posh restaurant and I had chicken soup, beef casserole and custard. We finished lunch and we went to the Paris airport to fly to Manchester for the big match.

We got off the plane and on to a coach to go to Old Trafford. We all went to the home dressing room so we could get our training kit on for the hour we had to train in. Once we had finished training we had loads of drinks, then we calmed down for the big match and we went to a restaurant in Old Trafford for tea, where we had a roast. Then we went back to the dressing rooms for a team talk because we were having a big match, after that we had drinks and biscuits.

At 19:00 the rest of the team and I went on the Old Trafford pitch for the last training session before facing Brazil in an hours time. At 19:30 we got our home kit on, it was five minutes before the match, we went out of the tunnel and onto the pitch for the National Anthems.

It was kick off - the ref blew his whistle.

At half-time we were winning 3-0. The Brazilians got 2 goals back in the second half but we won 3-2 and I received the *man of the match award*.

*Adam Oggelsby (11)*
*Grove Vale Primary School*

## A Day In The Life Of Victoria Beckham

7:00 I woke up, Brooklyn was crying.
David said 'Shall I go and calm him down?'
I said 'No, I will!'

So I went into Brooklyn's room, picked him up and took him into our room to his dad. He wouldn't leave David so I went and got him a bottle. Brooklyn wouldn't let me feed him, so I gave David, Brooklyn's bottle.

Whilst David was feeding Brooklyn, I searched through my wardrobe for something to wear. Finally I found something, my long black dress.

9:30 time to rehearse with the Spice Girls.

On the way I saw Mel C so I stopped 'Get in Mel I'm on my way to the studio.'

2:00 I got home, then David, Brooklyn and I went shopping. We bought Brooklyn the Man United kit and I bought loads of shoes, skirts and tops.

3:15 I sat at home and watched movies while David took Brooklyn to the nursery.

5:15 I went to fetch Brooklyn and he gave me the painting he had done for me and David.

8:00 We have either chicken supreme, spaghetti bol and lasagne but tonight we had chicken supreme.

8:30 Brooklyn was asleep in his crib.

12:00 Finally it was time for me and David to go to bed.

Goodnight!

*Carly Woakes (11)*
*Grove Vale Primary School*

# Rock

I got up and went for a shower, then I put my £100 velvet and leather clothes on, and then I went down to the fourth floor. I played on my Dreamcast, Smack Down. Then I went in my seven foot limo, to my servant, Carly Woakes I said, 'Take me to the Wrestling Federation Jabroni'

We got there and I was going to wrestle Stone Cold on Backlash. I beat him with a Rock bottom and then Undertaker came out to help me, then Kane came out and beat the hell out of the Undertaker.

I ran off but then Mankind punched me, he took me to the car park and he got a metal chair and he hit me, but I got up and hit him back, and I did the people's elbow on him, then I ran to my car and I went home.

When I got home the phone went, it was Vince McMahon he said 'You are the champion of the Wrestling Federation.' Then I went to bed.

By The Rock

*Thomas Niblett (11)*
*Grove Vale Primary School*

# A Day In The Life Of The Rock

One day The Rock got out of bed and went into the bathroom, had a shower and brushed his teeth. After that he went down the turning stairs and had his breakfast, and got ready for King of the Ring against HHH.

He slid into his limo and went to the studio and faced HHH in the middle of the ring.

The World Wrestling Federation Championship was on the line. They got into the ring and straight away The Rock got HHH in The Rock Bottom. The Game got a steel chair and hit The Rock on the head. The Rock went mental and did the Rock Bottom, and then the most electrifying move in sports entertainment.

1, 2, 3 The Rock was champion

*Sanchez Chatha (11)*
*Grove Vale Primary School*

## A Day In The Life Of A Teddy Bear

I wake up to find myself squashed up against the wall of my owner's bedroom. As if that wasn't bad enough, I have been awake all night with my owner tossing and turning. No one can get any sleep around here.

After I have been neatly tucked under the quilt, my owner goes downstairs. Finally, I am free to go to sleep, but not for long. A few minutes later my owner runs upstairs, she has forgotten me again, and has come to collect me. Now for my favourite bit - I get to ride in the car. Although pleasant, sometimes my owner insists on squeezing me and telling me what a 'pretty teddy' I am.

Eventually we arrive at our destination - Nursery School.

A big building crammed full of children screaming as if they were being chased round the room by a monster with a big stick. My owner approaches cautiously and I hide behind her back. Then I get dumped in the corner of the room as my owner goes off to play with some other toy. I sit until the end of the day when I am reluctantly picked up and dragged back to the car.

When we arrive home, I am sat up to the table, and have strawberry jam and other delights shoved into my mouth, but of course I am too polite to object.

After tea I am tucked up in bed with my owner and I doze into a restless sleep and then my day beings again.

*Naomi Shipman (12)*
*King Edward VI Camp Hill School For Girls*

# A Day In The Life Of Britney Spears

I stood armed with a hairbrush, the music blasted from the speakers, my make-up glowed. I was about to sing when my friend burst into the room and steals my act. My dreams shatter, I'll never be like her, the one I envy - the teenage superstar. I'm plain old me, a normal, average girl never to be noticed.

I see posters and turn a bright emerald from jealously. I wonder can I match her? Will I have sell-out gigs all around the world? Will I be branded a princess of pop? Will my friend ever shut-up? Which reminds me - has she gone home? Yes! Phew I can practise in peace.

I stand on stage. I feel a million dollars. I look at the crowd. The music blares - I open my mouth and hush descends over the crowd.

'The winner is . . .' I was nervous, my fists clenched, my neck sweaty beneath my shirt.

' . . . Ball!' I beamed I was Britney Spears. It may have only been a talent show I had won but I could do it. I was her, I was stunned into silence.

They asked me for autographs, I agreed. The fans get what the fans want! They wanted me to sing for a charity concert. I was living Britney's life, and I would be remembered for it. I was just longing to put my feet up though!

I lived her life in one day. The experience to last a lifetime.

*Louisa Ball (12)*
*King Edward VI Camp Hill School For Girls*

# A Day In The Life Of An Angelfish

The day begins with light filtering into the shallow waters of the coral reef. The angelfish wakes in its crevice, safe within the heart of the coral. His brightly coloured scales rippling as he swims to the entrance of his one night standing. He checks for danger, Moray eels curled up in their own holes and homes, waiting for prey to come within reach so he can strike out into the greeny blue waters. He swims guardedly among the brightly lit reef. He sees food and darts forward; he gobbles it up, every last scrap gone. Silently a hammerhead shark swims over the reef looking for a possible meal. Thankfully he has not seen the fish and swims away to another lookout to find food. The sun is rising and the rays beat down upon the water's surface, heating it to deliciously warm temperatures, as the middle of the day is near. A lionfish parades around the seabed, displaying his wonderful array of spines, dappled as the light distorts and jumps around nearer the surface.

More food is up ahead, but the fish can see an eel basking on the rocks nearby, should he risk it? He swims a little further forward, the eel stirs. No, today he will live and find food elsewhere. As the day draws to a close the fish looks for a possible sleeping place, finding one he snuggles down ready to begin a new day tomorrow.

*Emma Matthews (12)*
*King Edward VI Camp Hill School For Girls*

# A Day In the Life Of Appetite

My mother's head bumped lightly against my chest, waking me slowly. As I drowsily looked up, I saw the sun climbing the forest trees into the sky. I turned my head and looked towards the hills. The rest of the herd were slowly waking, and some were already awake and grazing. I staggered to my feet.

Later that day we moved further south. My mother and I stayed meekly near the end of the line, as I was still young and could not move as fast as the other horses. Near us, an old female was walking, dragging her heavy feet. She was blind and almost deaf. Another younger mare was in front of us. She was foaling and could not move very rapidly.

Soon we had crossed the plain and were nearing the stream. In the first few years of my life I had grown to fear deep and fast running water. However, I was relieved to see a small brook, its waters gently lapping the sides. I crossed with little trouble, taking a refreshing drink on the other side. We passed away into the depths of the New Forest.

That evening I lay down with my mother. I felt safe with the rest of the herd all around me. I slowly looked up to see the sun sinking into the amber sky.

*Amy Winchester (12)*
*King Edward VI Camp Hill School For Girls*

# A Day In The Life Of An Intellectual Snail

I crawl aimlessly up a rock for a few hours and eventually reach the top. My one leg feels like it's going to give in on me but I decide to carry on, just not as fast this time. As I trail slowly down the flat, boring rock, I think how meaningless life is. I mean what is there for a snail to do nowadays. I often sit upon my favourite 'thinking rock' back at the compost heap and try to work out the meaning of life. The only thing I've come up with so far is eating, sleeping and crawling (and that's if it's a good day)!

Sometimes it's depressing having such a high intellectual level of understanding, when I'm living with such ignorant imbeciles who just mope around all day. I do think they have a point sometimes though because is there really, truly, honestly, anything to achieve in the world today for us snails? The very lucky ones get picked for snail racing, but snails with a very high level of knowledge - for instance me, don't get noticed in today's society.

There's so much suffering in the world and no one realises what I have to go through in a normal day. Well, I suppose that's the disadvantage of being a snail!

Sidney (the snail).

*Kate Wilson (12)*
*King Edward VI Camp Hill School For Girls*

# A Day In The Life Of An Astronaut

Beep-beep, beep-beep, beep-beep, beep-beep I am awoken an hour late by the sound of my broken alarm clock ringing painfully in my ears. Of course this is not my call to get up, this is my call to turn over and think about getting up - or at least it would be if I wasn't strapped to the wall.

I guess I had better explain myself, I am one of seven astronauts chosen to go on a breakthrough mission to Mars. I can't say anymore now though, because I'm late. I'll answer your questions as I go along. You wanted to know the tough parts of being an astronaut, well to tell you the truth, I don't know where to start.

As I float through the living space (this is where we eat, sleep, exercise and spend any free time) I try to dodge Phil who is chasing his runaway breakfast round the capsule. My breakfast consists of many packets of dried food which you add water to and drink through a straw and if you knew what they tasted like, you would understand why this is one of the main tough parts.

Along with the difficulty of using the toilet and the gruelling fitness regime and confined spaces to live in. So you said you wanted to be an astronaut?

*Miriam Toolan (12)*
*King Edward VI Camp Hill School For Girls*

# A Day In The Life Of Upper Class Sheep

3am

I woke up to the sound of loud barking in the next field. Went back to sleep.

4am

Large nasty dog bit my prize-winning flank and rounded me up. Me . . . me! No one rounds up the Duchess Olivia of Snowdonia, I told that mongrel of a dog this, but not only did he ignore me, but he tried to sabotage my gorgeous fleece.

4.30am

I finally had to relent and allow myself to be escorted into the truck. It is hard to describe the difficulty of walking into a hole only fit for humans, with dignity. I managed.

5am

We've travelled away from my home and not one slave was left to attend upon me. I was most displeased, but the human who was driving had the nerve to make me stand upon . . . hay, not a cushion and not my usual red carpet!

7am

Tried to force down some of the common sheep feed, I was annoyed, I wasn't brought up in a house you know!

8am

I managed, I fell asleep again.

8.30am

A human came in holding a tube with a needle sticking out of it. He stuck it in my leg. It all went dark.

5pm

I was in this wonderful place. Oh look! There's a flying cow! Ooh! The world is swooping around.

5.05pm

I was sick.

6pm

I lay down, I went to sleep.

*Hannah Slade (12)*
*King Edward VI Camp Hill School For Girls*

## A Day In The Life Of A Goldfish

'Every day I swim around the corner and see amazing things I don't remember seeing before. Just now I swam round and saw a big monster like you staring at me. It's amazing! There is so much to see, I'm never bored or . . . I'm sorry, what was I saying? . . . Who are you?'

'They say you goldfish have a memory of only seven seconds!'
'Oh, is that so?'
'You were telling me what you do in a typical day.'
'I was? Oh, it's a brilliant place in here, it really is. I wake up, swim, swim, sleep and . . . Oh! I wonder what's behind this rock!'
'What do you mean, you've been swimming around it for the last hour?'
'I have most certainly not! Who are you anyway? Go away! Wow! What is this place?'
'Flippin' 'eck! It's a bowl! You've been here all your life.'
'I don't recall ever being here before.'
'Before what? Before 7 seconds ago? You are the most frustrating creature in the world. I'm off!'
'Oh hello! Nice to have a visitor for a change. Who are you? Here let me show you this incredible thing I just . . . What was I saying?'
'Aaaarrrrgggghhhh!'

*Anna Pugh (12)*
*King Edward VI Camp Hill School For Girls*

# A Day In The Life Of Jack

I'm Jack the gerbil, I've just woken up, Abi (my owner) has gone out to school and I'm stuck in my boring cage.

I eat a sunflower seed, I hate all those healthy green flaky things, I live on sunflower seeds and peanuts! Anyway, I mess up my cage and try to dig my way out of the glass, but end up squashing my nose.
'Someone's coming!' A strange face peers at me, I try to bite it,
'Ow!' The glass again.
Yes, they open my cage, pick me up. Oh no, I couldn't help it - all over their hand. I hear a female voice make a disgusted sound and then
'. . . Aargh!' she dropped me. I'm so scared, I run quickly past a giant foot and out of the door.
'Hey! I'm free, cool!'

I come to some steep bumpy things going down. I jump down one, loads to go. It takes me ages to get to the bottom and when I eventually get there, I was so worn out I needed a rest. I set off to find myself a comfortable bed.

I come to a very slippery floor surface. I wander along until I get to this cold shiny thing. It had this sort of round glass door, I jump through the door. Inside it's like my wheel, but gigantic. I find some soft things to sleep on and nod off.

I wake up to hear loud voices calling my name, someone is crying. I peep out the door hole, just then someone comes along and starts stuffing clothes on top of me. I squeal and jump out 'I've found him!' shrieked the person 'in the washing machine.'

It went dark, I smelt Abi's hands. Next thing I knew I was back in my cage. 'Oh well, I was hungry anyway. Now where are those sunflower seeds I buried?'

*Abigail Jennings (12)*
*King Edward VI Camp Hill School For Girls*

# A Day In The Life Of A Cat

A cat was roaming around on a hot summer's day, guarding her territory. Suddenly she spotted something, I wasn't sure what it was until she ran over to a big apple tree. On it you could just see the first apples starting to grow. I looked up at the tree and saw a squirrel scurrying from branch to branch, trying to get away from the cat below. The cat who was at the bottom of the tree, gave up and walked daintily away.

For a while after that, the cat (called Minnie) just walked around and chased bugs and flies. She gracefully settled down and slept for a while.

When Minnie finally awoke, she went inside and ate her food. A cat called Max came running up to her, wanting to play. You could tell that Minnie didn't want to play because she kept walking away. Just as she had settled down on top of an armchair, Max came running up to her and with his paw tapped Minnie on the head, trying to play. By now, Minnie was getting angry so she lifted her paw and whacked Max on the side. With this he ran off.

The next time I saw Minnie she was back in the garden, not chasing flies or bugs, but marching out a grey cat from the garden. It was almost like the grey cat (no idea of its name) had invaded her territory. The cat left, when Minnie spotted something . . .

*Tara Curzon (12)*
*King Edward VI Camp Hill School For Girls*

# A Day In The Life Of Skippy And Bounder

I opened one eye, I opened the other. I sniffed and I smelled trouble. I sniffed again and I distinguished the smell of fire.

'Ahhh! Fire! Fire! Fire!' I shrieked getting louder and louder each time as I glanced behind me seeing roaring flames dancing and leaping out of control, swallowing huge amounts of bush in great bursts. My heart pounding I retreated and fell backwards over Bounder.

'Youch!' he squeaked waking up from a deep sleep (I think he was dreaming about flying dogs, but that's beside the . . .)

'F - f - fire!' shouted Bounder, leaping at least 20 feet into the air.
'What are we going to do? We're gonna die!' He said in a panic-stricken voice leaping into my arms kicking and screaming. He is a younger kangaroo than me, and at times he can be very juvenile. Well okay, I'm panicking like crazy too, but I don't let it show. I glanced back at the fire again. It was getting closer. Bounder looked back over his shoulder and jumped off me (at last!). I turned round and then it hit me, we were trapped! The fire was coming at us on one side and in front of us the fence enclosing Mr Doo's farm.

If we jumped the fence he was sure to shoot us. That's what happened to my good friend Digi. I was going to take a chance. I jumped the fence and hopped for my life. The end of the fence is in sight now. Nearly there . . . Then I remember Bounder!

*Kirsty McGuff (12)*
*King Edward VI Camp Hill School For Girls*

# A Day In The Life Of An Ordinary Boy With An Extraordinary Tale

It was a dull and boring Monday morning. Mum woke me because I had slept through my alarm.

I told her I was sick, weak and dying. She didn't fall for it, so I dragged myself out of bed and I slowly got dressed and had breakfast. By the time I was ready to leave I was late, really late. I dashed out of the house and down the road. I reached the bus stop just in time to see my latest possible bus turn around the corner. I cursed myself for being so lazy, I had to get up on time in future. I began to think up my excuse as I waited for the next bus which would get me to school, twenty minutes late.

A large black limousine pulled up and a stout man stopped out, followed by a man I immediately recognised as *Will Smith!* All the girls wanted to meet him and the boys wanted to be him. Wouldn't I be popular if . . . ?

He walked over and introduced himself. He asked me if I needed a lift or was I happy getting the bus? Has this guy ever taken public transport? I jumped at the chance. On the way he talked about what it's like being a singer/actor. The journey ended too quickly when we arrived at school the chauffeur opened the door and I waved goodbye as my excitement faded.

No one believes me, but you do, right?

*Leigh Salsbury (12)*
*King Edward VI Camp Hill School For Girls*

# A Day In The Life Of A Budgie

I am Emily's pet budgie Jill. I'd better say a little about myself. I am four years old and I live with Emily's parents, Emily (obviously) and her four year old sister, Sarah. At the moment it's 5am and I cannot sleep. I fell out with Jack yesterday after an argument. I thought it was my turn on the oh sorry! Swing, but he was oh, convinced it was his turn. We argued for a long time before I said I wouldn't speak to him anymore. I don't think I can keep it up for long though as I'm getting a bit tired and oh bored. Actually I think . . .Zzzzzz!

Hello again! Sorry about falling asleep during our conversation. I think I'll ask Jack if we can be friends again? Okay, deep breath 'Um, Jack! Jack, can we start speaking again? I'm sorry!'

Now I know when humans speak to birds they appear to listen but never reply. This is because birds do answer humans, but to you it sounds like a chirp. Your voice sounds exactly the same to us, but we understand you. 'Um, well okay then!' Jack replied.

'Ahh help! Our cage is being invaded by a big green monster! Heellpp meee!' I shouted.

It has landed on the breeding box. It hasn't moved. It's just sitting there. Emily's just pushed it forward. It looks familiar, it's . . . Lettuce! Mmm this is nice. It can't be . . . It is!

It is oh 8pm and I'm very tired. Well it's been very nice meeting you. Bye zzzzz.

*Emily Johnson (12)*
*King Edward VI Camp Hill School For Girls*

# A Day In The Life Of A Hamster

It's 6:30pm, I guess it's time to wake up. I clamber over the wall of my house. Yes, great my food bowl has been filled. I make a desperate dive for the nuts. Delicious, hmmm! I guess I should take some to store under my bedding. So I fill my cheeks and head back to my bed. Right, I feel thirsty, I run along to my water bottle. My tongue reaches out and I feel a large drop of water fall in my mouth. Light comes on, hurting my eyes, in comes a large, dark figure, who opens the cage door.

Yes, fun time! I run halfway up the steps next to the cage door and wait eagerly. A large hand comes through the door and I jump up on it. I love the feeling as she holds me close cupped against her chest. Hooray, she's putting me in the ball. I jump inside and as soon as the lid is placed on, I run away. Out of the door of one room into another, going behind chairs. Man, I love running!

No, don't stop me I'm having such a great time.
She takes me out, back into my cage. Oh well, I go to my wheel and carry on running and running so much I lose track of time.

I'm tired, I climb back into my cosy bed and fall asleep peacefully.

*Lucy Scholes (12)*
*King Edward VI Camp Hill School For Girls*

## A DAY IN THE LIFE OF DAVID SMITH'S BRAIN

Dream - theme tune: Da, da, da, d, de, de, you get the point?
Brain left, Section 3, Part Dreamworld, Box 3b, 'Will never happen!'
Set: In America New York. Hero: David Saving: Blonde, 5'8 size 8
From: Gangsters, Strong gangsters, gangsters with guns, big guns and sunglasses.

1, 2, 3 action holding blonde on the top of an abandoned building for no apparent reason at gun point. David comes flying in and . . . falls flat on his face. Intruder alert trespassed into room threatening to drag you out of bed stating that you are late. You remove your head from pillow, look at Aston Villa clock 8:00, school starts at 8:30. Still need to get dressed. Mum refuses to give you a lift. Life is not fair and never seems to go your way. Shove (what looks like your uniform) on, pick up bag, shove any obstacles out your way, route out the house six year old brother playing on stairs with Action Man (Upp! Not really Action Man any more, head happened to fall off!) Older sister having her breakfast, nope not hers, yours, stuff it in mouth, wallop from sister. Err marmalade, spit it out on to sister's plate before confronting mum run out of the houses, keep running, you think you've lost her.

Now 8:30 school is fifteen minutes down the road, run and you'll make it in five (give a pathetic (classed) as a run). School gates approaching, glance at watch 8:26 he walks into the school and . . .

(Will he survive the headmaster - find out in the next edition).

*Genevieve Ewing (12)*
*King Edward VI Camp Hill School For Girls*

## A Day In The Life Of A Poor Child In A War

A day has just ended and another is beginning, the child awakes and hopes that a miracle will happen. He hopes for the meal of his life but sadly his wish hasn't come true. His face will never dwindle. For hours upon hours he sits and rocks backwards and forwards, his mind wandering far away for he does not know where his family is. He can hear the gunshots being fired. The screams of the people being attacked, and of those whose houses are being burned.

He wonders if the day will come when peace is declared. He daydreams and imagines he lives in a mansion and he is the richest boy alive.

He changes the sound of gunshots to trumpets and his hunger into a full stomach. He licks his lips and fingers and imagines he has just had the meal of his life. He walks around looking for little droplets of water to quench his thirst, hoping he won't step on the deadly landmines - hoping, hoping!

Suddenly, he hears footsteps, he darts behind the wall, hands shaking, his breath rattling. He thinks his life is drawn to an end. The door behind stands ajar, should be risk it? Is it worth it? Yes! Anything is better than death. He stays there shivering, beads of perspiration breaking on his brow. He hopes tomorrow will being good luck!

*Shivani Shah (12)*
*King Edward VI Camp Hill School For Girls*

## A Day In The Life Of A Pound Coin

'Hi! My name is Penny. I was born in 1983 in a coin factory. I got my name when I was mistakenly put in the penny section. Whenever other coins call me Penny I say 'Wrong again! You're 99 pence out!'

Now where was I? Oh yes, at this particular moment I am in a purse. Although I wish that I could see everything going on outside.

Ah! What's happening, I'm bouncing up and down and everywhere. Stop it right now! Bet you thought I was going to have a metal attack (for humans similar to that of a heart attack). Hey, I can see daylight. This isn't the person that took me out of the money jar this morning. Unless my eyes deceive me, because I certainly don't remember seeing four young boys. I get it! This purse must have been stolen. Oh no, I'm rolling out 'Cling!' Not again, I hate being on the floor where people trample all over me.

'Oh Mummy look! A pound coin, can I take it please?' A filthy little chubby hand comes down to grab me. Now I open my eyes and I am in a sweet shop 'Can I have a candy stick and a handful of cola bottles?' 'Certainly!' says the shopkeeper 'that will be 60p please!'
It is now time for me to be handed over to the shopkeeper.

Back in the till I go and wait for another adventure!

*Shivani Tandon (12)*
*King Edward VI Camp Hill School For Girls*

## A Day In The Life Of A Chicken

I woke up and opened my eyes and met the gloominess around me. The sky was still dark and my barn was filled with frost and the hay around me was frozen. All of the other chickens were asleep.
'Cockadoodledoo!'

Everyone soon got up and rushed past me.
This was my last day to live. I heard the other chickens talking about it
'Oh, she's going to be roast tomorrow!'
I knew my turn to be killed would come someday, but not this soon!

First you get cut by the farmers in the throat and . . . you get cooked!
I saw it with my own eyes. My mother was killed and I was there to see it all happen. She was in pain and she looked at me and whispered
'Bye!'
'Mommy, mommy!' I screamed.

I decided to eat my breakfast, which was cold, almost frozen.

My so-called friends were outside playing and laughing. They didn't care about me, they just felt sorry for me!

The clock struck 12; two more hours to live. I decided to spend my last sacred hours sleeping in my spot hoping I would never wake up again.

The clock struck two. The farmer came and fetched me. I've loved this world more than anything. My whole life rushed past me but now I'm sure I will be reunited with my mother.

*Faiza Fazal (12)*
*King Edward VI Camp Hill School For Girls*

# A Day In The Life Of A Rabbit

Hi! My name's Rocket, Rocket Rabbit. I come from a pet shop, but then this family came and took me away from my brothers. I had sisters as well but they were kept in the next box. Anyway, this family came and took me to their house and that's how I got here. I have much more space now than before, but I have another rabbit sharing it with me. She's called Rachael, Rachael Rabbit. She has been here longer than me.

Anyway, I was woken up this morning by a banging noise. I found out from Rachael that this noise happens every time the children need to go to school. After a while, the children had gone and the noise stopped, everything was quiet.

I was hungry so I hopped out and there was food a few hops away from the door. I ate and drank some water. Rachael said she'd show me around. When I'd stretched myself a bit, Rachael came out. She nibbled at the door, then it opened.

She lead me to a door and pushed it open, she showed me a big black box which was called a Television and she told me that children fight over it. Rachael turned it on, it was very relaxing and I soon fell asleep.

'Rocket, wake up!' I woke up. My brother was staring at me,
'Guess what?' he shouted 'you've been chosen!'
'Yeah! These children are buying you!' shouted my older brother.
I wonder if they have another rabbit!

*Chrissy Wong (12)*
*King Edward VI Camp Hill School For Girls*

## A Day In The Life Of A Cat

I woke up in the morning and it was freezing cold. It was a very dull morning. I was starving. I needed something to eat. My owners had taken me for a walk and then left me there. If I was with them I would have milk and cat food. 'Oh someone have pity on me please!'

The humans were mumbling something, then the ladies smiled and picked me up and took me home. They gave me food and milk. Oh they were so nice, well at first they were but later they picked me up and threw me out of the window. I got hurt really badly. A cat went past me, she looked at me and she seemed lonely. I decided to speak to her. 'Miaow.' Our conversation went on, she told me how she had been treated.

We made friends and had to steal anything decent we could to fill our empty stomachs. After an hour or so, a large man walked past us. Then he turned around and walked straight to us. Cattie was terrified. He tried to pick us up gently. I found him nice but Cattie tried to scratch him but I just managed to stop her. It was a long journey. Soon we reached a small but cosy house. The man fed us and tucked us into our baskets.
'Night Cattie!' I said.
'Night, night Catsie' yawned Cattie.

*Bushra Jahangir (12)*
*King Edward VI Camp Hill School For Girls*

# A Day In The Life Of . . . Rocky!

'There he is!' I whispered excitedly to the pups. 'Get ready 5, 4, 3, 2, 1 *Post!*' We snatched the letters through the letterbox, nearly snatching the postie's hand off and successfully squashing my nose. The letterbox clanged shut and I squealed with pain as my nose got stuck. The pups rolled over laughing, all except Weiler who was trapped under the Daily Mail. With my nose squished in the door, I could definitely smell a familiar scent. I sniffed again to make sure . . . It was Sydney! 'Quick you lot, round the back, Sydney's coming.' I managed to free myself from the door, with Rot and Weiler's help. (After Weiler had freed himself from the newspaper) 'There he is!' said Rot. 'On the fence again' Weiler added.

'As soon as he jumps off that fence into our garden go and get that posh, pampered Persian and mess that neatly groomed fur up.' Sydney jumped and the pups, all five, Rot, Weiler, Stone, Ben and Jake ran and pounced with their muddy paws, making Sydney's fur look more brown than white. 'Oh no, not you pestering puppies again - Rocky, can't you keep these little ones under control?' Sydney asked (What a cheek!) With that, Sydney trotted off, back to next door. 'Well done you lot, that should teach him not to trespass on my lawn.' Now, I'm in the mood for a snack. 'Come on you puppies, I'll teach you how to get food off the work surface without getting noticed.'

*Laura J Davies (12)*
*King Edward VI Camp Hill School For Girls*

## The China Doll, A Real Trouble

There was a girl called Sarah, she was very young. She liked dolls but she had just moved and left her old doll back at her old house, as it was very tatty. She begged her dad for a new one.

Later on that week, her mum, dad and herself went shopping, they bought her a new doll, except they didn't realise that it was a China doll.

The night of Hallowe'en came and Sarah and her two friends, Lydia and Zara, were coming over and staying in the attic. They stayed up all night but that was after 'trick or treating'.

In the morning they woke up and tried to get out of the attic but it was no use, the China doll had locked the door in such a way that they didn't know it was locked, they thought it was jammed.

They had enough food to survive while they thought of what to do. The next day her mother tried to let them out, but unfortunately it was no use.

Zara had thought of a really good idea. They all did exactly that. It was to connect the old clothes in knots and try to escape through the window. They all escaped safely. Soon her mother realised it was the China doll, so she burned it.

*Sema Latif (12)*
*King Edward VI Camp Hill School For Girls*

# A Day In The Life Of My Grandad

'Beep, beep, beep, beep.' My grandad turned the alarm off. 'It's 5:-- and it's time to get up and go to work,' he said to himself. He got dressed and went to work. In his hand he had a suitcase and inside it was clothes that he had made himself. He arrived at the first block of houses and knocked on the first door. A woman came out with a baby in her arms. 'Would you like to buy my warm, comfortable clothes? I have a variety of colours and sizes,' said my grandad. 'No thanks!' said the lady. He went to a couple of other houses and he managed to sell only one or two garments. He moved on the second block of houses and knocked on all the doors. He managed to sell most of his garments. It was 6:0pm and he was exhausted but he had to carry on because he was only halfway through his job. At 10pm he managed to sell all of them. Then he walked back to the home that he shared with a friend that had flew over to England in 1957. Grandad had something to eat and went straight back to work, which wasn't selling, but making the clothes that he had to sell the next day. He made fleece tops and he made trousers and other garments. He finished about 12:00 and then he went to sleep. The next day he walked 16 miles again, trying to sell the clothes.

*Parul Kenth (12)*
*King Edward VI Camp Hill School For Girls*

# A Day In The Life Of A Mouse

Now that he was full up, the mouse cautiously tiptoed to the edge of the table. Almost straight away he drew back, gasping in horror at the sight of the evil, hissing, black cat, which had retired to its favourite position, underneath the table. The mouse quickly recovered from the shock and then he thought of a cunning plan. He slowly pushed a bowl of apples (which were on the table) to the smooth circular edge. And with one last hard shove, pushed it over the side. The glass bowl, in which the apples were kept, hit the hard, wooden floor with a smash. The apples fell out, hitting the cat with a dull, sickening thud. The mouse jumped off the table, the cat's soft fur breaking his landing. He hurried towards his hole, but couldn't resist stopping to grab a large piece of cheese lying nearby. As he stopped to heave the heavy piece of cheese onto his back. A hard, merciless paw slammed over his head, preventing him from seeing anything. He panicked and started to bite and kick the dark walls around him. The cat lifted its paw in a moment of pain and the mouse rushed off to freedom and his hole. Sadly though, he tripped over his long, skinny tail. The cat behind him gave a miaow of triumph and then it pounced . . .

*Christina Cheung (11)*
*Manor Primary School*

## A Day In The Life Of Myself

I always go to school. I learn a lot at school. I learn how to do my times tables. I do lots of PE. School is great! I do my reading at school. I have a great teacher, her name is Mrs Wellings. Every morning we have an assembly. We have a topic, it's called plants. We are learning about how plants grow. We found out that plants grow from tiny little seeds. I enjoy learning. I like my friends. At school I saw this girl named Amanda. She's my bestest friend ever. My favourite lesson is art and craft. I like to do PE, that's my second best lesson. I like talking to my teacher and friends in the playground. I play with my friends.

*Sophia Hamid (9)*
*Moor Green Junior School*

# A Day In The Life Of Britney Spears

At the Ritz Hotel in London, Britney rose from her slumber. She had a big day ahead of her, shooting her new video. She had thirty minutes to get ready. She called for a limo and got in, all ready for her new video.
'Where to Madam?'
'Virgin Recording Studio.'
She was there within the click of the finger. In the middle of recording her mobile went off. It was Top of the Pops saying they wanted her to come and do her new song. She agreed, for her fans' sake, rather than her own. She did her song, signed a few autographs and left.

To her surprise, when she got home her mom was in the hotel Britney was staying at. 'What are you doing here?'
'I was shopping in town and I thought I would pop in.'
'Oh' she replied.
'So can I stop over?'
'Yes, sure Mom'
Britney said 'Night' to her mom and fell asleep. After about ten minutes of sleep she awoke because she saw a flashing light and wondered what it was. It was one of her fans with the press, wanting photos for the article being wrote.
'What are you doing this time at night? You've woken up my mom. Now be quiet and don't come back.' Britney said in a stern voice.
'Bye' she said and slammed the door in their faces.
'Once again, night Mom!'

*Tara Roleston (11)*
*Moor Green Junior School*

# A Day In The Life Of Victoria Beckham

8.00am Vicky woke up for a full day's shopping. First she cooked breakfast for her and David, then got changed. A while later she said 'Goodbye' and went out. You see she was getting married in two days time and needed to fetch her wedding dress and buy some new shoes.

First she had a snack of a packet of crisps, biscuits and a chocolate bar. Then met Jennifer Aniston up town, because they were closest friends and Jennifer wanted to see what she was wearing. Vicky and Jennifer went into the dress shop and everybody was staring and waving. After she got her rose-white dress (£700) and left as quickly as possible. They went looking in the shops, like Tammy (Etam), New Look and after 3.00pm she went to fetch her wedding shoes. In the shop Victoria looked at so many pairs of shoes. After half an hour she finally picked the wedding shoes that looked the best (for £75 they should be).
They had a meal at McDonald's and then went home. She took Jenny to the train station because she was going to see her mom. Then Vicky went home to David and as soon as she got in I can tell you she fell straight asleep.

*Olivia Sutton (10)*
*Moor Green Junior School*

# A Day In The Life Of Julia Roberts

8:10 Dear Diary, it's just another normal day in my life, the door won't stop banging with the press and I can't even walk down the shops to get a bottle of milk without everybody staring at me. Film takes start at two-thirty and I'm hoping to get an hour's rest beforehand.

1:55 As I stepped out of my creamy white limousine the noise of all my hysterical fans whistled into my ears and rattled my brain. I couldn't even hear myself think. When my manager pulled me into a building I was glad to be in an environment where it was not a novelty to these people to be in the same room as me.

You know being famous is not all hip because your privacy is always being invaded. I never have time for my family which are always my number one priority. On the other hand there are advantages with being an actress, I mean, I know I moan about my fans but without them there would be no point. They make me feel that I am a good actress. With being an actress there are always mixed emotions, you have to take the good with the bad.

See you tomorrow.
               Julia.

P.S Don't forget film shoot's at ten and late lunch at 4, again.

*Loretta Cummins (11)*
*Moor Green Junior School*

# A Day In The Life Of Ricky Martin

It was 9:00am Ricky Martin got ready to go to the first place he'd ever been to, it was America. It started like this.

We arrived at the airport in a long, silky, black limousine. A man in a navy blue suit opened the car door for Ricky Martin. Out came Ricky's right foot, followed by the left. Crowds gathered and screams from fans crept into his ears and surrounded his brain.

As Ricky Martin walked into the building, shielding his face from the cameras, he noticed a young girl around 18 years of age standing patiently waiting for Ricky Martin to notice her. Ricky did and walked straight past the screaming fans and went up to this girl. Ricky, whose real name is Enrique, said 'Excuse me I've been allowed one fan to come on tour with me, and well, you look like a nice person, so would you like to come with me?'
'I would, but, but . . . Oh go on then, but I have to be back by tonight, 7:30. I'm an actress for Miami Seven you see.' She stood up and linked arms with Ricky Martin. Her name was Hannah. As they strolled in they began to hold hands tightly. She told Ricky Martin she had a band called S Club 7. Ricky Martin heard Hannah singing and she was very good, in fact she was so good she was sent a record contract from Ricky's record company the next day. Ricky went to watch Hannah act and then went for a meal with her. By now Hannah and her band mates were famous, just like Ricky Martin, but Ricky fell in love with someone else and they were parted.

The press were informed and tried to interview Hannah and Ricky. But when they realised they wouldn't say anything to impress them, they came up with their own front page story. Hannah and her band have remained famous and are planning to stay that way for a little longer. As for Ricky, well he's got a concert on the way and is on tour with a jolly man named Stewart.

*Louise E Langan (11)*
*Moor Green Junior School*

# A Day In The Life Of . . . Michael Owen

Hello this is Michael Owen and I am a professional footballer for England and Liverpool. My managers think I am quite good for a 21 year old. I'm playing against Germany today, so I have to do a lot of training so we will beat them. Hopefully, we will.

Meanwhile the match was starting and I was very nervous. The whistle blew for the first half. Kevin Keegan was determined to beat Germany at least once. A goal up in the 53rd minute. Alan Shearer headed it in the team were ecstatic.

Now Germany were trying their best. They nearly scored a couple of times but they needed to train more every week. Finally, the final whistle blew and they were ready to party all night for two days. Kevin Keegan was very pleased with his squad.

*Kieran Conlon (11)*
*Moor Green Junior School*

## A Day In The Life Of Julia Roberts

Dear Diary,
7:15am. Hi, it's me again, I've got to rehearse for a show tonight, the show rehearsal starts at 7:30pm, so I have got a couple of hours to myself. I need to go shopping but I just cannot stand the crowd of people asking for autographs and photos. I mean, the other day I was in a shop and about 15 people crowded around me, all of them wanted my autographs and some of them took photos of me. It is so rude of them and so embarrassing.

9:00am. The show normally takes about 10 takes but today is a bad day, so it will take about 25 takes. Sometimes some of the actors are late so the shoots start at 7:30pm but they ask us to be at the studio at 7:00pm.

12:30pm. I am just about to get into my lovely bubble bath but I have got to let it cool down, so I have a little bit of time to write. The show I am rehearsing for is Notting Hill, I am not going to tell you anything but this is a little bit rude and it is very funny as well. My bath must be cool, so I will carry on writing when I get out of my bath.

1:45pm. I have just got out of my bath and I have freshened up but I am really dreading the rehearsal tonight. A lot of the rehearsals I don't mind but this one is not good. I can tell a lot of the time when things are going to be bad and when things are going to be good. I have got to go to the shop and it will take quite a long time because of all the people crowding me and asking for autographs and taking photos of me.

6:45pm. I have just got back from the shop and I have got 2 minutes to write, then I will have to leave to go to the studio.

10:55pm. I got back about half an hour ago. I have had a shower and I have freshened up. The show took 36 takes because of silly things, like I had the wrong clothes on or my hair looked wrong and things like that. Anyway, I need to go to bed because I have got a long day tomorrow. I will write back soon. Bye.

*Jasmine Fennell (11)*
*Moor Green Junior School*

# A Day In The Life Of Victoria Beckham

Dear Diary,
Hi, it's me again, it's a special day today. Yes, it was the Cup Final and Man U won. There was an enormous, huge, magnificent party downstairs. I'll tell you later about the football match but let me tell you about the day.

This morning, David wasn't here with us, he was with the team on their way to the football match. Me and Brooklyn went after. First I changed Brooklyn into a Man U shirt and trainers that his dad was wearing, it was so cute, I had to take a photo. I changed into my real leather top and trousers and got everything ready for the football match.

Before the match started I phoned David and said 'He will do his best.' He is really bold, he is definite that he will score a goal.

I am really proud of the two men in my life, David and Brooklyn. David's been working hard for the football match, usually at 7.30 he would wake up and do his morning jog. At 2.30pm me and Brooklyn arrived at the football match.

The team were practising some football moves. As David noticed me he ran up and gave me a kiss and gave Brooklyn a hug.

At 4.30 the match started, the first goal was scored by Andy Cole and everyone cheered on. The second was scored by Giggs.

The opposite team were Germany drawing 2-2. We had 5 minutes left and someone had to score.

Suddenly there was only 2 minutes left and Giggs had the ball, passed it to David and David scored and then the time ran out and Man U won.

I was so happy, I'm starting to cry now. It was so amazing, astonishing. The fans cheered and after the team came over and had a party.

We had beer, wine, music, food and the team, the party finished at 1.00am in the morning. Luckily Brooklyn is asleep now, it's 3.00am in the morning, I'd better get to sleep.

See ya!

*Abeeda Pasha (11)*
*Moor Green Junior School*

## A Day In The Life Of Me

I woke up at 7:30 and I go to the toilet, wash my face. I have toast for my breakfast and a drink of milk. My dad goes to work. I wait for my uncle to come to fetch me to go to school. I get to school and go to the playground and play with Ameer, Daniel and Jack until the bell goes. We work until lunch time, when I have my school dinner. I don't like them. After school I go to mosque until 6:30m when I go home. I have my dinner. I usually have a jhapatti, beans and rice and a drink of milk. I watch some television and I go to bed at 9:00.

*Wasim Hussain (9)*
*Moor Green Junior School*

## A DAY IN THE LIFE OF WHITNEY HOUSTON

I woke up and heard bipp, bipp, bipp, bipp then I heard brr, brr. I picked it up 'Hello hi ya I've changed the plans, we're not going to have a talking show, we are going to have a gig' she said quietly. 'What' I said loudly. I put down the phone. I went downstairs and got a drink of orange juice and had a bowl of Special K. After that I put the shower on and took my clothes off and got in the shower. First I washed myself and washed my hair. Then I found myself singing I Will Always Love You. After I went to practise my songs, I went to my room in the practising parlour. Amber my manager walked in.
'Good you're practising. It's twelve o'clock and the gig starts at seven,' she said. 'Where is it' I said.
'USA'
'What? We better be going then' I said. We drove very fast to the airport. When we finally got there we saw our flight was just about to go. 'Quick.' We sped across the runway and got there just in time. We boarded the plane safely and were on our way. When we got there we went straight to buy some clothes for the gig. After that I went to practise. Then it was time to get ready for the gig. I got my clothes on and brushed my hair back and got in my Limo. We drove off. When I got there we walked up the back alley. When I got in I sang. That was the end of the day.

*Kay Wilson (9)*
*Moor Green Junior School*

# A Day In The Life Of Louise

One day I woke up and looked at my clock. It was 11.00am. I had to rush into work. It took me two hours to get there. I had to be in at 12.00pm. I put my foot on the brake. I was going really fast and then the police were after me. I had to stop. I nearly crashed. I slammed my brake on. Because I stopped my car, my car broke down so I phoned my boss and said 'I can't get to work, so I will be late. My car has broken down.' So I went home and saw my family. They dropped me off to work. I had to work longer than I usually do because I came late. That was the end of my day so I woke up the next morning and got to work on time. My car did not break down.

*Stacey Rhodes (9)*
*Moor Green Junior School*

## A Day In The Life Of A Deer

One day as always the sun was shining and my mom was giving birth to me. I was frightened because I could not run or I could not walk. So she had to teach me. Later I could walk and I could run. At night-time I heard a rustling noise. I saw a cheetah. I bellowed *'Run.'* Everybody woke up and ran. They ran into a little group. The cheetah saw us running so he ran after us. Then he saw a baby buffalo and ran after her. I ran out of the group to save the baby buffalo. I butted the cheetah with my head. He ran away. Then me and the buffalo girl were friends until the day we died. Me and my friend the buffalo baby grew up together and we died when the day came.

*Hayley Sanders (9)*
*Moor Green Junior School*

# A Day In The Life Of Nicky

On the 16th June it was my birthday. I was going to be twenty. I woke up in the morning and couldn't breathe and phoned my mom. I got rushed into hospital. All of a sudden I woke up and I saw a wonderful man, but it was strange because I always dream about him. He took me home and I lay in bed and fell asleep. The next morning I washed my face, got dressed, brushed my teeth and put my make-up on. I work as a waitress. I served 170 meals. I got home at 12.00. I washed my face, brushed my teeth and combed my hair. I woke in the morning and said 'I will phone my boss and say I won't be coming in OK.' I got into the bath, washed my hair and got dressed. Then I brushed my hair. Then the doorbell rang. It was the man from the hospital. He came in and asked me if I wanted to come out tonight at 7.00. I said yes. I washed my hair, curled it, brushed it. The clothes I wore were a silver skirt up to my knees, a silver belly top, with silver boots and coat and belly button chain. I went into my silver sports car. Then I pulled out my silver mobile and said 'Where do you live?' '00 Stirchley, Birmingham.' I went straight there.

*Kerrie Fox (9)*
*Moor Green Junior School*

## A Day In The Life Of Alan Shearer

One afternoon I was on the way to work. I was just getting in my car and I heard the phone ring. I got out of my car, opened the front door. I answered the phone. It was my mom. I said 'I've got to go.' I said bye and drove off in my car. I drove to work. When I got there I got changed into my shirt and shorts. It was twenty minutes away. Before the match I was very excited. It was the final of Euro 2000. It was England V France. By this time it was only ten minutes away. We were just coming out. As we came out the people were clapping. The whistle went for kick-off. The whistle went for half time. The score was England one France nil. I scored. We came out for the second half. There was only two minutes left and we were winning 2-0. I scored both of them. The whistle went. We had won it. I went into the dressing room to get changed. I drove home in my car. When I got home I thought it was a good time to go to bed. In the morning I had a lie in till about 11am. It was very nice.

*Billy Woodhurst (9)*
*Moor Green Junior School*

## A Day In The Life Of A Swimmer

One morning I woke up. It was lovely and sunny. I forgot I had to go to work so I got dressed, brushed my hair and had to wash my face. Then I was ready to go to work. I went and got in the car. The manager said 'You are late. You were supposed to be here twenty minutes ago.'
'I am ssso sorry.'
'It is OK, now get your costume on and get in the pool.'
'OK' I said, getting my swimming costume on. 'I had a bad day.'
'Don't worry and get dressed and you can go home.'

When I got home I made myself a cup of tea. I sat down drinking it, then I fell asleep. When I woke up my cup of tea was all over me. I got up, cleaned the chair and then got my clothes off. Then I went upstairs because I was tired. All I heard was the water of the swimming pool. The water started to come through the walls. It started to flood, then it covered my face. I shouted 'Help me.' No one heard me. I wasn't to be seen.

*Kerry Doak (8)*
*Moor Green Junior School*

## A Day In The Life Of Paul Scholls

I get up at 7.30 for training with some mates. Then, time arrived. It was time for the big match, England Vs France. France took kick-off. Beckham my team mate passed to me after dribbling and I shot and I scored. By the time it was half-time I had two hat-tricks. We were winning. The score was 6-0. We started training again for half-time. Next half begins. Vierra scores on the French team with a great header. Ince, my team mate passed to Beckham, to me . . . blast! What a goal, in fifteen minutes of the half. In a few minutes Ince headed to Beckham and with great power and energy, blasted the ball to the goal and a wicked goal was accomplished. After two minutes the game was going smoothly until blast . . . we were drawing. They had scored with fifteen minutes left. In time, Ince took a shot. The goalie saved it. We were angry. We were running out of time. Then the penalties - Beckham took first, what a goal, then Vierra's turn. He took a shot but our goalie Seaman caught the ball. I took the next shot and goal! When the game ended the score was 13-6. Then we celebrated 'cause of our great victory and excellent cap. All thanks to our great player Paul Scholls and increasing practise by Kevin Keagan and our great cheering crowd for confidence in ourselves but the greatest players were Beckham and Ince. But man of the match was Paul Scholls.

*Inderjit Ramm (9)*
*Moor Green Junior School*

## A Day In The Life Of Britney Spears!

I get up at 7.30. I'm still really tired. I exercise then for about an hour. I do stuff like go on the stepper etc. Then I practice song lyrics and dance routines for an hour (boring!) Now it's dinner for half an hour. Then my most important part of the day (my concert). I love all the people cheering and seeing them rocking to music, dance and singing. I also get elation inside me because of the singing and dancing. Now I've just completed my concert and it's 4 o'clock. Now I'm going home to freshen up before I go to see my boyfriend. I put on my favourite dress and set off. We either go to a restaurant or watch a movie. I don't often stay up late because of all the rehearsals and things like that. We watch hour or two hour movies. We often enjoy them but sometimes we don't rate them as much as other movies. Sometimes we just talk about our busy day. Then I have to part from my boyfriend and go to bed. I really don't want to leave him. After that I sleep in my nice comfy bed and think how lucky I am. Also I think about all the hard work I have to do tomorrow or any different days.

*Lisa Titshall (9)*
*Moor Green Junior School*

# A Day In The Life Of Britney Spears

It was very early in the morning and the noisy phone rang. I woke up and picked up the phone. I heard 'Get here now at work quick' and I dropped the phone, got dressed and my mind was in a muddle because I had lots of things to do. Then did a slice of toast, buttered it and ran out the house, slamming the door behind me. I opened the car and reversed off the drive, choking on my toast as I did it. Then I finally got out into the road. When I got there I walked into the building and they marked me in reception and I went through into the big hall. There was lots of lights on the stage and there was music on, but then I realised there was one thing missing, me of course ready to rehearse for tonight for a show that I'm doing and I had to go on the stage and rehearse, so that's what I did. I sang 'Hit Me Baby One More Time' and when that was over I had my lunch. I had chicken and chips with tomato sauce on my chips. Then it was time for me to perform in front of a live audience. I was very nervous when the curtain opened and then it was over. Then I said goodnight and I drove home in my car and had a good night's sleep for a long time.

*Emma Thorpe (9)*
*Moor Green Junior School*

## A Day In The Life Of Billie Piper

I woke up extremely excited, it was my first concert. I was going to sing my latest single (Day And Night). I went downstairs, my mum was standing with her hands on her hips.
'You took your time' she said,
'Oh I haven't got time for your lecture,' I snapped wearily.
'Here's your breakfast.'
'Oh no I hate egg Mum, why do you always make it for me? I'm not going to eat it' I said. I poked my egg with my fork. Then I had an idea. I called my dog and I fed him my egg! I watched as he scoffed it down.
'Oops I am late for my concert Mom'
'But -'
'Bye Mum.'

I jumped into my Mercedes Benz convertible. I rode at 100 miles per hour. I finally reached my venue and I started to shake as the curtains lifted up. I had my best silver and black dress on. Suddenly the crowd jumped up and down cheering; as I walked to get ready for my first act called Day and Night. The concert went really well. When I had finished the curtains went down and I just got a glimpse of my boyfriend. Then I knew nothing would stop me from my future concerts.

*Roxanne Ali (9)*
*Moor Green Junior School*

# A Day In The Life Of Britney Spears

10.00am The alarm goes off 'Get up now' so she gets up and goes out to the studio to shoot some more of her songs. She did Oops I Did It Again and some other songs for her new album and then she says 'Stop one minute. What is going on?'

12.00am She goes out to get something to eat and all her fans run up to her for an autograph and she says OK who's first and they say 'Me.' 'Me.' 'Me.' So she sees a girl who looks sad. So she says 'You're first' then she goes into a cafe and they all say 'Oh please can we have your autograph?'

*Leanne Jones (10)*
*Moor Green Junior School*

# A Day In The Life Of Britney Spears

It was 8.30 on Tuesday 6th July and I had just woken up, I was meant to be up an hour ago. I rushed downstairs to put the toast in and ran upstairs to have a quick wash and get dressed. I packed the stuff I needed for the day and ran out of the house before the toast had popped up. My drive to the studios was quick (probably because everyone was nearly at work).

As soon as I got into the car park I ran through the doors and into the studio and it was only 8.50. I went and got my clothes on, then onto hair and makeup. The whole video took five hours.

After that I had to go to a signing. There was about 3000 people there. I was there till 5.30 I got home at 6.00. As soon as I got home I had a cheese sandwich and went to bed.

*Aisha Malik (11)*
*Moor Green Junior School*

## DAY AND LIFE WITH WILL SMITH

Dear journal I have woken up once again at 6.30 in the morning. Starting a new video for my song Wild Wild West waking up at 6.30 in the morning is just hell. My wife moans at me every time I get up. I just wake up at six because it is dark, so we can get a perfect spotlight.

I have let out about five or six albums. The only day off I get is when I call in sick. My boss is really grumpy. The best song I have released so far is 'Do You Want Me To Freak This' and the best album is 'Willennium', but my best singer is Jay-Z. He is a much better rapper than me.

By lunch time I feel real tired, so I go home, have a really light lunch and have a little rest. By then my wife comes back from work. Then I have to go back to work shooting the new video for my song.

I come back from work about 12.20 in the night. So I only get six hours and ten minutes' sleep. I get a vacation every two years but I still get no peace. I go to Birmingham and as soon as I step off the plane, cameras were up in my face and videos in my face, so I can sign them. I just wish that I never became a singer or a movie star. I hardly get to see my kids or my mom or my relatives. So all of that is my everyday life.

*Aaron Lammy (11)*
*Moor Green Junior School*

## A Day In The Life Of Del Piero

Once upon a time there lived a man called Del Piero. He was a football player. He had a pet called Zola. One day Del Piero went for a walk in the park with Zola. Del Piero let Zola fly around. Zola was amazing. He flew to fetch a fish from the pond to eat at home. When they had cooked the fish they took the bones out and ate the fish and drank cola. One day they went shopping on their horse and zoomed and bought all the staff they wanted. Zola bought a bird cage for himself. Del Piero bought a T-shirt with the Rock on it. One day Del Piero put it on and showed off. He was happy and tired. When he got home he ate some biscuits with tea and then when Del Piero went training with Zola Del Piero said he should be in the football team side. Del Piero side in the park with Zola. When Del Piero got home Zola saw a track outside Del Piero's house with a sign of pounds. Del Piero went outside.

A man outside said 'Here's your money, because you won the Lottery,' 'Yes I did win the Lottery.'

So he took the money and went inside to have tea and biscuits with Zola. Del Piero lived happily ever after.

*Karanvir Shergill (8)*
*Moor Green Junior School*

## A Day In The Life Of Alan Shearer

One day I got up at 5am. I had a big match for Euro 2000 against Germany today. I packed up my England kit and went to Wembley Stadium in my car. When I got there there was all the other players training for the match. Then I started to train. At 12am me, the other players and Kevin Keegan had some lunch. At 2pm we got our kits on again and went onto the pitch with the Germans lined up beside us. We sang the National Anthem. I had David Seaman on one side of me and on the other side I had Gary Neville. When we were finished singing me and Paul Scholes took kick-off. I raced up the pitch. David Beckham kicked it up the pitch but it went off. It was a goal kick to Germany. Their goalie kicked it down the pitch. One of their players had got the ball. He crossed it to another player. He had a shot. He missed and it was a goal kick to us. David Seaman kicked it up the pitch. It went on a bit like that all through the first half. When we got into the changing rooms we all had a drink and some of us had something to eat. Germany took kick-off and then I scored and we won one nil by my goal.

*Christopher Gumbley (9)*
*Moor Green Junior School*

# A Day In The Life Of A Swimmer

I woke up on a morning I felt like swimming. I was in luck because we went swimming that day, I never noticed people were calling me Nikki. I went in the deep part of the pool. Everyone kept on coming up to me saying 'Are you going to have a race?' 'No I'm not a swimmer!' I said. Just then I looked in the mirror tiles. There was something unusual about my face. I was a swimmer called Nikki. I went up to the person and apologised and said I will have a race. I had a race. I let him win because he wasn't as fast as me. After that I went home and there was a letter for me. I opened it and I was supposed to go to a tournament, but I rushed down there and I told them that I'll do the race. I got in and told the others good luck. I waited till the starter said 'Go.' I swam and swam as fast as I had ever swam before. I had won after that. I had to go home. At home I was worn out. I went to bed after I watched the end of Friends. I went to sleep. In the morning I got out of bed and went downstairs, looked in the mirror and I was myself again. That day we went swimming again and I couldn't swim as fast as I swam when I was Nikki.

*Danielle Rhodes (9)*
*Moor Green Junior School*

## A Day In The Life Of Martin Grainger

Dear Diary,
Martin Grainger is a football player for Birmingham football club. He gets up at five o'clock and goes to training at six o'clock. He is training for the play offs to get in the Premiership.

The day finally came and all of Birmingham City players were nervous. Birmingham were playing Barnsley. The referee blew the whistle. Barnsley kicked off first after twenty minutes. Barnsley scored a goal, and after thirty-five minutes they scored again. It reached eighty-five minutes and it was 3-0 to Barnsley and suddenly bang 4-0. They scored again.

The whistle blew and all of the fans had gone except Barnsley fans. When Martin and the blue boys got in, Trevor Francis, Birmingham's manager went crazy. Then Martin muttered under his voice said 'We're knocked out. Maybe next year.'

*Wayne McVeigh (11)*
*Moor Green Junior School*

# A Day In The Life Of Lennox Lewis

I was in a boxing match against Evander Holyfield. 'Round one!' yelled the referee. Dinga-linga-ling! rattled the bell, the match had begun. Evander struck out at me *smack!* I was hit over to the other side of the ring. He tried again but he missed and I came back with an uppercut. Evander stumbled, this was my chance. I jumped up and gave him ten jabs. He landed on the corner. He looked like he was in a coma. I walked over to him suddenly. He opened his eyes and jabbed me in the gut. 'End of round one' exclaimed the referee. We went to our corners to get a drink and a towel. We drank and wiped ourselves. Dinga-linga-ling rattled the bell, I hit Evander with a right hook. His nose bulged with blood and water spurted out of his eyes, I hit Evander with one more uppercut. He landed on the floor unconscious. '1, 2, 3, 4, 5, 6, 7, 8, 9, 10 Holyfield has lost Lewis is the winner,' bellowed the referee. He gave me a sparkling belt. The cheer of the crowd was invigorating. I walked out of the arena holding my belt and the crowd cheering 'Lennox' they chanted. Next I went to film an advert. At the studio the crew had already set up. I waited until it was my line. 'You need a quality drink to quench a big thirst' next it was narrator's line. 'Tango the star's favourite drink' the advert was over, at home I leaped into bed after an exhausting day.

*Kieran Davis (9)*
*St John Fisher RC Primary School, Coventry*

# A Day In The Life Of David Beckham

My name is David Beckham. I have a little son called Brooklyn and I have a wife called Victoria, I love her very much. I go football training every day. I mostly play on a Saturday but I am off on a Sunday. I sometimes go modelling during the week. On my football boots I have Brooklyn sewn onto them.

I am sponsored by Adidas because they make my football boots. Last week Romania knocked us out of Euro 2000. I feel sad because we didn't win. Alan Shearer is going to retire from England because he wants to see more of his family but he is still going to play for Newcastle.

I haven't fallen out with any of my team mates. When I am off on a Sunday I go to mass in the morning with Victoria and Brooklyn. After mass we go to see my mum and dad. We go on a Sunday because we are busy with things. At my mum and dad's house we have lunch.

Later on we go down into the countryside and we take Brooklyn to the farm. Brooklyn likes the sheep and the lambs very much. Afterwards we all went into the forest. We showed Brooklyn the birds in the sky. When we got to the end of the forest we saw a park and a little club next to it where we had dinner.

Me and Victoria watched Brooklyn play in the park. Later on, we went back to my mum and dad's house to get the car. We drove down to Victoria's parents to see if they were OK. Brooklyn went into their back garden and went into the swimming pool with me and Victoria.

When we go anywhere there are always cameras. We do not like being photographed, only sometimes. If we shout at someone or are nasty it is in the papers or on the news the next day.

*Laura McGrath (9)*
*St John Fisher RC Primary School, Coventry*

## A Day In The Life Of William Shakespeare

I, William Shakespeare the great have just written the greatest play ever, Romeo and Juliet. It is a tragic love story about two families who hated each other, but there is a sad ending. I'm going to the public house with the man in charge of the theatre, to show him my play. 'Hello, over here William!' shouted a round tubby man with brown hair and looking very cheeky. I knew he had been here a while because of the amount of glasses on the table. I handed him the play.
'What will you be drinking?' he asked me.
'Mead, please.' As soon as I said it, I got some. After twenty minutes and an hour he emerged, with tears in his eyes. 'I will show it on the 21st next month,' he told me.
'Thank you!' I said happily, off to the hairdressers. Now a bunch of drunken hooligans came in ranting and raving. 'Better get out fast,' I told myself. Off to the hairdressers.

I'm at the hairdressers. Time to go in, there's a lot of people in here.
'Who am I after?' I asked.
'You're next, Sir' he replied.
'Humdily dum' and it was done
'Shilling, Sir,' so I gave him one. I never knew how famous the play would be.

*Ryan Gillespie (9)*
*St John Fisher RC Primary School, Coventry*

## A Day In The Life Of Ryan Giggs

Hi there, I'm Ryan Giggs. You might already know I play for Manchester United on the left wing. I'm squad number eleven, I'm twenty-six years old and I was born in November in Cardiff. I spent sixteen years there until I signed for Manchester United. My mum and dad divorced when I was young. My mum's surname was Giggs and my dad's was Wilson. I went to live with my mum. When I became a footballer I decided my surname was Giggs.

The things I do in the day are: have my breakfast, get dressed, brush my teeth, walk my dog, go to the cliff and spend four hours' football practice, sign some fans' autograph books, before I go home for a shower, have an interview with Goal magazine, go to have a meal with my girlfriend Davena, sometimes we invite Beckham and the two Nevilles around for a swim or a game of pool, then we go in my Jacuzzi, we have a few drinks, while we watch the new James Bond movie, The World Is Not Enough. It's getting late so my guests leave. It's a great life being a footballer. It can be hard, like when I have an injury. It's my day off tomorrow so I can have a lie in.

I'll have to go now. I hope to see you at one of the matches this season coming up. Do you think we will win the premiership this season? I do. Yorke will be the top scorer again with approximately twenty-five goals. I'll have to go now, see you soon.

*Phillip Hall (9)*
*St John Fisher RC Primary School, Coventry*

# A Day In The Life Of Robert The Bruce

In the year 1314 there lived a famous Scotsman called Robert Bruce. I was in line to be the next king of Scotland, but the English invaded Scotland and took over the country. They put in place an English king called Edward I. I had an army who fought the English in many battles but always lost.

One day I looked out of my tent and saw half of my army was dead. I was fed up so I went to a cave to think. When I was sitting I saw a spider spinning a web on a wet rock. It fell nine times but the tenth time it made its web. I thought if the spider can do it I can keep trying to beat England.

I gathered my army and marched to Bannockburn, to fight the English. The English charged but they sunk in the marshes. The Scots fired their bows and arrows and killed the English with their broad swords. Me and my army chased the English over the border. That night the Scottish army celebrated and I told them the story of the spider.

Scotland remained free for four hundred years because of this famous day. People still tell the story of Robert the Bruce, and the spider which means 'If at first you don't succeed, try, try, again.'

*Liam Jordan (9)*
*St John Fisher RC Primary School, Coventry*

# A Day In The Life With Damon Hill

My name is Damon Hill. Each morning I get up at 8.00 and have my breakfast. For breakfast I have egg, sausages and beans. After breakfast I take the children to school, then I go to a gym and I do swimming to keep fit. I go to meet my friends for lunch. Their names are Lee, Sam and Jerry. I like to eat pasta because it is good for me. I get interviewed a lot on TV and for magazines. Today the local school has invited me to open their fête. I buy my wife some flowers most of the time. I pick my children up from school and go to a local park to play football. After I took my children to the park, I told them I had a surprise for them. We drove to a local garage and I picked up my new car which was a Porsche, which reminded me of my racing days.

*Luke McAleer (9)*
*St John Fisher RC Primary School, Coventry*

# A Day In The Life Of Kevin Keegan

This morning I woke up not having slept very well, because I couldn't stop thinking about the game against Germany tonight. We have to win this game to stay in the Euro 2000 Championships. I was disappointed in the last match, we lost 3-2.

After breakfast, I took all the football players on to the training field to have a warm up and to tell them who would be playing in the team tonight. It was a hard task because we have got to win. All of England's fans would be watching and expecting great things to happen.

There's only an hour to go before kick-off and I'm giving the last chat, telling them they have to win, be strong in defence and try to take your chances in front of goal. The hour is up and it is kick-off time. I am on the touch line encouraging my team to do well. It's half time and still nil-nil. I went into the dressing room and I was telling them where they were going wrong. Back on the touch line, we've got a free kick, David Beckham takes it to Alan Shearer, he heads into the net. There is only two minutes left and we are still winning one-nil.

The referee blows the whistle, we have beaten the Germans after 34 years. I am so happy I feel like a hero. I go into the dressing room to congratulate the players and I think I will sleep better tonight.

*Richard Taylor (9)*
*St John Fisher RC Primary School, Coventry*

# A Day In The Life Of John Hales

My name is John Hales and on the 22nd July 1531 Queen Elizabeth The First came to stay at my house in Coventry. She stayed for two days and nights. I was excited but nervous as well. She came on a brown horse. Her servants came too, also on horses. One of the horses was pulling a cart carrying six large chests.

As she entered the garden I rushed to the door and opened it eagerly. I found her on the doorstep, smiling, her white teeth gleaming. I bowed to her. She was wearing a cream dress with red roses. She had a cream ruff with necklaces, rings on every finger and pearls in her hair. I welcomed her in and then I went out to put her horses into the barn. When I came back in Queen Elizabeth was standing in the front room making faces at the chairs in there. It was obvious she thought they were dirty so I took her outside into town and we climbed the spire of St Michael's Cathedral. I pointed out most of the places I knew in Coventry.

When we came down the Mayor stopped us and he gave Queen Elizabeth one hundred gold coins sent from nearby villages. When we got back I thought about the next day. It was going to be very exciting.

*Sinead Docherty (8)*
*St John Fisher RC Primary School, Coventry*

# A Day In The Life Of Walt Disney

One morning in 1922 I got up so early because the premiere of my Bambi Film was being shown that night. I was tingling I was so excited, I could barely keep my feet on the floor. The chef made me egg, bacon, sausage, toast, tomato and beans. I was thrilled with him. A big breakfast on an important day.

As soon as I got to the studio me and my staff got working straight away. Instead of having a normal break. I decided to treat them all so I took them all out for a posh meal. We all ordered. I had jacket potato and for dessert I had cheese cake, it was scrumptious.

Anyway work finished and we all set off to get ready. I skipped and jumped all the way upstairs to get ready. The phone didn't stop ringing while I got ready. My friends were wishing me luck. So it was very hard to get ready, but in the end I managed.

I arrived in a big limousine. Everybody was clapping and cheering, cameras didn't stop flashing and lots of people were questioning me. I could barely hear myself think. I got into the cinema at last. When I was on stage I had to introduce myself. I said, 'Good evening everybody, this is my new film called Bambi and I'd like you to sit back and enjoy.'

The film had begun. Half way through the film there was an interval I had a beer. The beer was just what I needed. We all went back in the room to continue the film. After the film was over we all had a celebration. We had a disco and I had a little dance for fun. That was a day I'd remember and never forget. I sat back and thought how lucky I was.

*Jolee Gavin (9)*
*St John Fisher RC Primary School, Coventry*

## A Day In The Life Of Lady Godiva

I woke up at 9 o'clock but I was still tired. I'd been awake all night thinking about what my husband, Lord Leofric, Earl Of Mercia, was doing. I knew he was making everyone pay too much tax and they were very unhappy about it.

I felt bad for the people so I asked my husband to reduce the taxes but he refused to listen. All night I thought about making him listen.

Later I told my husband, 'I'm going to protest against you until you lower the taxes.'
Lord Leofric replied, 'I'll lower the them on one condition, which is you have to ride around the streets of Coventry on a horse. But that isn't all you have to be naked!'

I was scared at first but I remembered I had very long hair and I knew it would cover me. I told everyone to shut their windows and blinds so I was happy when everyone did.

I was still nervous but I had to stand up for what's right. Luckily my hair did cover me and no one looked out of their window. Suddenly I saw a man looking out of a window. I screamed and panicked so I just went past as fast as I could without looking back and then got my clothes on and went home.

At home I found out that the man was called Tom, and he became blind when he looked out of his window at me.

Lord Leofric reduced the taxes.

*Nicola Gormley (9)*
*St John Fisher RC Primary School, Coventry*

## A Day In The Life Of The Queen Of England

Hello, this is Elizabeth Windsor speaking to you, HRH Queen Elizabeth II. My lady in waiting has just brought my breakfast with a selection of newspapers and magazines to read, I do hope they have written nice things about me today.

My clothes are out ready for me. There are four sets, I don't know which I shall wear. I will have to wait for my personal dresser, she always tells me which looks best. Now what else is happening today. My hairdresser is due at 10.00 am and the Prime Minister at 12.00 am. I do hope it doesn't take too long, as I have to take the corgies out for a walk later.

My children Charles, Anne, Andrew and Edward are coming later in the afternoon. We are all going to talk about my mother's birthday in August. She will be 100 years old then, so we have to sort that out between us. I hope that it will be a really super day for her. My husband Phillip and I are having tea with her later.

Finally, myself and Prince Phillip have been invited to a dinner in aid of one of my many charities. It isn't a very posh do so I have told my jeweller that I only want my diamond necklace and bracelet not the tiara tonight. I have told Phillip to let me do all the talking because he always says the wrong thing. Then after the dinner, I can go to bed and read a bit of my Barbara Cartland book.

*Natalia Costa (9)*
*St John Fisher RC Primary School, Coventry*

# A Day In The Life Of Aaron Southan 2132

Aaron Southan wakes up at 7.35 am and tells his computer to get him dressed and clothes materialise on his body. He then asks for jam on toast, it appears on a plate in front of him. He eats it while watching his personalised news. It tells him his teleportation system is ready and to get to work by 9.00 am. Aaron looks at his watch and says, 'It's time I'm off to DOUS.' (Development of Universal Spaceships). Aaron walks over to his teleportation system and it teleports him to work.

At work he meets his best friend Michael Jenkins who is on the brink of helping Earth colonise Pluto. Aaron goes over and helps Michael confirm the blast-off of the specially heated radiators. At the same time Aaron's boss phones from the newly colonised Alpha Centurai. The boss tells him to see whether Aaron and Michael can do anything to help them make solar-powered spaceships. Aaron puts forward the idea of extra-sensitive. The boss says that that may be it. By that time it was already dinner time.

When Aaron got home he was tired so he got out his PlayStation and played his Civilisation X. He was extremely tired so he went to bed and had a wonderful dream.

*Luke Southan (10)*
*Yarnfield Primary School*

# A Day In The Life Of Me

When I wake up I brush my teeth. Sometimes I go to the dining room to have my breakfast, then I go upstairs to change from my pyjamas into my school uniform and then I comb my hair. This is the time I get the warning from my mum, to say how late I am. I run as fast as I can to put on my shoes and pack my bag. By this time my big sister and my small brother are waiting for me in my dad's car. I quickly grab my coat and run out into the car.

When my sister's in her school, my dad rushes the car towards my school. I meet my friends and then our teacher takes us to the classroom. We work hard for two hours and then it's playtime. We return to the classroom for maths for at least an hour. Then we usually do silent reading for fifteen minutes and by then it's time to have our dinner. When we are called in we go to the hall to eat and then me and my friends play. After that we have two hours of education.

I then return home to have my bath and do homework. To end the day I watch TV, brush my teeth and go to bed.

*Aliasgher Hassam (10)*
*Yarnfield Primary School*

# A DAY IN THE LIFE OF AN EGYPTIAN

Egyptian men would wake up very early, to get ready for work. Men wouldn't have a nice posh clock, oh no! Their wives would have to wake them up. Men would usually work on a farm or be a slave building pyramids.

Women would cook the dinner, which would not be a lot. Maybe just a handful of corn. I wouldn't like that but in those days there wasn't a lot to choose from. The women would grow seed. If men didn't work hard they wouldn't get any food for the family and they would get whipped if they were too slow and lazy. Pharaoh the king of Egypt, in those days anyway, would call the slaves weak and thin, ragged people.

The slaves would build about half of the pyramid but would have died by the time it was finished as it took about one hundred years to build. When the men had done a hard day's work, if it was good work, they would have food for their wives to cook for them and their children.

In those days life was not easy, it was not a life I would like to live. I don't know about you but I'm glad I was not born in those days.

*Katie Turner (10)*
*Yarnfield Primary School*

# A Day In The Life Of A Teacher

A teacher has to get up really early to get to school. Sometimes teachers have to loudly shout at naughty children and sometimes they are really nice to some kind, sensible children. Teachers teach all kinds of lessons like maths and English. Some teachers go home early and some teachers go home late because they have to mark lots of books. They go to bed very, very late after marking all those books.

*Toni Lee  (10)*
*Yarnfield Primary School*

# A Day In The Life Of Myself

Today, I went to Cannon Hill Park to feed the ducks, it was fun. Then they started to follow us. I went to the play area and made a friend, her name was Anna. We were mostly playing on the fireman pole. I jumped from the top and she could not. I loved playing in the play area with her.

Then I went to my nan's for dinner we did not have it straight away. I played in the front for a bit then I had my dinner. I had lamb, cauliflower, mashed potato and cabbage. Then I was watching Eastenders, it was a repeat, I had seen it before. When we had finished watching it all we went home. We sat down for a few minutes, then I went to get in the bath and had a wash and washed my hair. I got out of the bath. Then I was playing with my brother Luke. I was playing with a ball that you have to roll to each other.

When it came to 6.00 pm I had my supper. I ate it up so I could get back to doing my homework, the quicker I do it the more time I will get to play games or watch television and not go to bed because I don't want to spend the night doing this. I do want to spend some time with my family because I love them so much.

*Emma Sloggie (8)*
*Yarnfield Primary School*

# A Day In The Life Of David Beckham

The life of David Beckham is a lot of fun to hear about, because of all the football bits. He is very famous and is married to Posh Spice, who is also famous because of her singing, so they are a rich couple. I think he could play better than he does if he tried. In England v Portugal he played very well. I think he should have scored though, but you don't have to score to play well.

He looks kind on television. I think he would be even kinder if you saw him in real life. He is one of the best free kick takers in the Premiership.

He hasn't scored many goals but tries to. I think him and Paul Scholes are the two best players in Man United's team. He looks really young and I know he is, but I don't know how old he is. Do you know how old he is?

He does like children, because at the beginning he puts his arm round one. I am not a big fan of Man United but I like him because he plays for England.

Beckham's wife is kinder than Beckham because she likes children more than him. Do you know where he lives? I don't.

*Mark Butler (9)*
*Yarnfield Primary School*

## A Day In The Life Of A Victorian Orphan

My name is Mary Scott, my mom and dad have died so I am an orphan. I am eleven years old and I live in Nantwich in Cheshire. I have to work in a dirty, untidy cotton mill.

Each morning I wake up at 5.00 am which is very early and I have my breakfast which is porridge and bread. I get dressed in a frock, stocking and an apron and start work at 6.00 am which is very early. I make clothes for the boys.

During the day I pick up cotton from the floor, mend broken threads, fit new bobbins and brush the machines.

For lunch I have pork or beef with potatoes. For a drink I have milk or water and for Sunday lunch as a treat I have a mug of tea.

At the end of the day I have my tea, go to school then I go to bed.

My favourite day is Sunday because I have my Sunday dinner and I play instead of school. For church I wear a green cloak and the boys wear green T-shirts. If you steal an apple or do something naughty in church you will be punished.

*Sam Slattery (9)*
*Yarnfield Primary School*

# A Day In The Life Of A Victorian Orphan

My name is Mary Scott. I live in Nantwich, Cheshire. My mother and father died when I was eleven years old. I am very lonely. I work in a cotton mill. I have got two pairs of stockings, two frocks and two aprons, also two vests.

Each morning I wake up at 5.00 am. I get dressed into my stockings and a vest and a frock and my apron. My work starts at 6.00 am. I like it at the mill, it's fun. My friend's name is Annie, she is very nice.

During the day I pick up cotton from the floor, brush the machines and clean them down at the end of the day. I fix threads and put new bobbins on when the old ones are empty. I work really, really hard. It's tough work.

For lunch I have pork and bacon and water. I like my dinners. They are really nice. For Sunday lunch I have beef, potatoes and tea that is my favourite.

At the end of the day I go to school on week days. It is good learning because I am with my friend Annie. Annie is my best friend. I am good in school, I learn a lot and it is good fun.

My favourite day is Sunday because I can play with Annie. We have a treat, beef with tea. Annie and I play lots of games. It is good fun. We do lots of work as well. We write, read and colour. Our teacher is really good.

*Aileen Brady (10)*
*Yarnfield Primary School*

# A Day In The Life Of A Victorian Orphan

My name is Mary Scott. When I was eleven I became an orphan. I lived in Nantwich. My mum and dad died. At that time I was wearing rags, then an important man said, 'Go and work in the cotton mill.'

When I went to work at the mill I was given two pairs of stockings, two aprons and two vests. They were all wrapped in a brown paper parcel.

Each morning I wake up at 5.00 am for my 6-7.00 am shift. My friend Annie usually wakes me up.

During the day I mend threads, fit new bobbins and pick up cotton from the floor.

At the end of the day I clean the machines. I then have tea which is pork or bacon with potatoes and play with Annie and Bruce and then at 10.00 pm I go to bed.

My favourite day is Sunday because I play lots of games if I am good. I have beef and potatoes with a mug of tea as a special treat. We go to church and I get to say the prayer at the end and then play lots more games like *Snakes and Ladder, Pass the Parcel, Guess Who, Hide and Seek* and then brush our teeth and go to bed.

*Aaron Evans (10)*
*Yarnfield Primary School*

# A Day In The Life Of A Victorian Orphan

My name is Mary Scott. I live in the town of Nantwich in Cheshire. I am eleven years old. My mother and father have died. I am an orphan and I have nowhere to live and I need food and clothes.

The Law said that important men and women in my town had to look after orphans, to give them clothes and a home. I have found a good place and I get money but I need to work for my food and clothes. I work in a cotton mill.

I pick up cotton from the floor, sweep the floor at night and put new bobbins on the machines. I go to school on three nights in the week with my friends. We play *tig, hide and seek, cards,* and *snakes and ladders* and then we go to bed.

I hope to leave the mill when I am 18 years old. I want to have eight children when I get married. They will have to work at the mill too but they will not be orphans. They can come home at night and go to bed in my little house.

*Jason Bassett (10)*
*Yarnfield Primary School*

## A Day In The Life Of A Victorian Orphan

My name is Mary Scott, my mother and father died when I was eleven years old. I work in a cotton mill. I pick cotton off the floor, I put new bobbins on the machines when they are empty.

Each morning I wake up at 5.00 am and I get ready for work at the mill. I have my breakfast and I start.

During the day I mend broken thread, brush the machines and so on and make clothes for the boys.

For lunch I have pork and bacon and I have milk and water.

At the end of the day I go to school and I come back to the big house to go to bed.

My favourite day is Sunday because I go to church to pray.

*Sireena Bibi (9)*
*Yarnfield Primary School*

# A Day In The Life Of A Victorian Orphan

My name is Mary Scott. My mother and father died so I am an orphan at eleven years old. Since my parents died I have had to work in a cotton mill. I used to live in Nantwich which is in Cheshire.

Each morning I wake up at five o'clock for work. I start work at eight o'clock. When I get up I have porridge and bread with water. I get my work clothes on then go downstairs to go to work.

During the day I pick up cotton from the floor. Mend broken thread, brush the machines at night. I put new bobbins on the old pieces of thread. Sometimes I like working but sometimes I don't though.

For lunch I have pork, bacon with potatoes and a drink of water. I think it is quite nice. Sometimes I have milk. At least I have a nice meal at the end of the day. It's nice.

At the end of the day I finish work at about five or six o'clock. I come home and have something else to eat. I get my bed clothes on and go to bed.

My favourite day is Sunday because I have beef and potatoes for lunch and some tea. We get to play in the evenings.

*Kirsty Meddings (10)*
*Yarnfield Primary School*

# A Day In The Life Of A Victorian Orphan

My name is Mary Scott. I am an orphan because my parents have died. I am 11 years old. I live in the town of Nantwich in Cheshire. I had nowhere to live when my mother and father died.

Each morning I wake at a cotton mill at 5.30am and get ready to go to work at the mill at 6.00am. I work in the cotton mill making clothes for the boys. I also mend broken threads.

During the day I work in a cotton mill making clothes for the boys. I picked up cotton from the floor, mend broken threads and put new bobbins on the machines. I enjoyed it.

I have pork or bacon and potatoes for dinner in the week. I enjoy my dinners, they are very tasty. I especially like the pork, it is very tasty. I sit with my friend Annie.

At the end of the day I go to school to learn. I like school it is the best school I have ever been to. It is a night school - it is the best school ever.

My favourite day is Sunday because it is my favourite dinner. I have beef and a mug of tea. It is very nice and I can also play. It is very good.

*Adam Curtis (10)*
*Yarnfield Primary School*

## A Day In The Life Of A Victorian Orphan

My name is Mary Scott. I am very poor so I have to work in a cotton mill for my food and clothes for me and boys. I live in the town of Nantwich in Cheshire. I am very lonely. I am only an orphan.

Each morning I wake up at 5 o'clock or earlier. I have my breakfast. As I go to the cotton mill I receive two vests, two aprons and two pairs of stockings. I like the cotton mill. I'm glad I found it.

During the day I pick up cotton, mend broken threads put new bobbins on machines and brush machines.

For lunch I have pork or bacon and milk or water for dinner. It is really yummy. It isn't my best meal but I still like it.

At the end of the day I walk home with my friends. I really enjoy it, we talk about what we did at work and secrets about our life. It's a bit noisy.

My favourite day is Sunday because the dinner I have is beef and a mug of tea. We play games at the cotton mill. We only have half a day but I still want a whole day. My life is perfect at the cotton mill. At the end of the day I go to school.

*Narinderpal Singh (10)*
*Yarnfield Primary School*

# A Day In The Life Of A Victorian Orphan

My name is Mary Scott. My mother and father died when I was eleven so I had to be an orphan. I had to work in a cotton mill. I have to work there for food and clothes.

Each morning I wake up at about 5.00am to 5.30am in the morning. When I get dressed I wear my vest, my stockings, my frocks and my apron I have to live with a special man.

During the day I pick up cotton, put new bobbins on the machines, brush the machines, fix broken threads and I brush the floors. I make cloths for myself and the boys.

For lunch I have potatoes, pork, bacon and water. I have lunch at 12 o'clock. I have dinner with all the other children. I like the pork the best. I love my dinners!

At the end of the day I go home and I lie down and have a rest. I go to school in the evening. When I go home from school I go to bed and go to sleep.

My favourite day is Sunday. I have my favourite dinner, my Sunday dinner and I get to play with my friends. For my Sunday dinner I have beef, potatoes and a mug of tea. I go to church and it is very good.

*Liam Jelfs (10)*
*Yarnfield Primary School*

# A Day In The Life Of Bill Gates

Bill Gates gets up in the morning, has his breakfast and drives to Microsoft. When he gets there he looks at Windows '95 and '98 and thinks how he can improve them. He has a brainwave - Windows 2000.

He calls a meeting for all of the senior staff to discuss their ideas for Windows 2000. They all come into the meeting room, and sit down at the table and open their folders to discuss Windows 2000.

After an hour of talking about Windows 2000, Bill starts to design the new logo for it.

He can't understand why the monitor keeps switching on and off on his PC which he is working on. He realises that every computer has switched itself off. 'What shall I do?' he thinks to himself.

He tries to switch the computers back on. Nothing happened. Bill gets worried, none of the computers will work. So he goes to the Microsoft factory next door and picks up 15 computers, trashed the ones that did not work and sets the new ones up.

The time it took him to set the computers up it was time to go home. So he got his bags drove home and had sweet and sour chicken for his dinner. He played on his computer for a bit of time and then went to bed.

*Adam Brinkworth (9)*
*Yarnfield Primary School*

# A Day In The Life Of Van Gogh

Van Gogh is famous for his paintings which he drew of different buildings, people and places. He mostly drew portraits of people. Here is a list of some of his paintings; The Church of Averues, The Starry Night, Irises and The Old Peasant.

Van Gogh inspired me because of his brightly coloured paintings. On the day that he drew the Church of Averues, I think he got out of bed, called room service and asked them to cook him some bacon, eggs, beans, tomatoes and sausages for his breakfast.

Then I think he got his coat and went out to look for something to draw. He came to a church, stopped and then found a spot to put all of his things. He looked carefully at the church before starting to draw it. He'd look at the church again and decide where to begin. After he'd finished the painting I think he would have gone to find out the name of the church.

Once he'd found out the name of the church Van Gogh would write it on the back of his painting. Finally he would go to a restaurant and have sausage and chips for his dinner. I think he'd finish off his dinner with a cup of tea and a game of pool.

Before going to bed Van Gogh would cut off his ear and send it to his girlfriend.

*Emma O'Neill (9)*
*Yarnfield Primary School*

# A Day In The Life Of Orphan Mary
# A Victorian Girl

She woke up at 5.00am every day. Around her she saw a room full of girls. First she saw her friend Anne, because Anne woke her up. She had porridge, milk and water for breakfast. After breakfast she went to work for thirteen hours.

At work Mary broke her finger on a machine so she could not fix bobbins, fix broken pieces of cotton or pick pieces of cotton off the floor at night. The only thing Mary could do was pick up pieces of rubbish on the floor.

Her friends made her feel really happy when she was sad and a part of their group.

She felt tired every day because she woke up early and worked hard for thirteen hours and went to school for an hour.

At 7.30pm she had her evening meal. Today she ate bacon or pork with potatoes, milk and water.

Then she went to school to learn how to write on sand and slate. Then she learns to read the Bible. 'You're a very smart girl,' said the teacher.

Finally, she then went back to the dormitory in the big house and then fell asleep until 5.00am as she was exhausted.

This is a day in the life of orphan Mary.

*Craig Jelley (10)*
*Yarnfield Primary School*

# A Day In The Life Of Orphan Mary - A Victorian Girl

I wake up at 5.00am everyday. People are nice at this mill. Around me I see loads of beds full of orphans, 2 to each bed. It's very hot in the beds. I have a breakfast of porridge, bread and water.

After breakfast, I go straight back to work, I find it really tiring and very boring, but I have friends and love.

All I have in the world is 2 pairs of socks, 2 frocks, 2 aprons and 2 vests. It was very embarrassing but some of them didn't even have that so I tried not to worry about it that much.

One day as I was working on the machines I caught my finger in the machine, I nearly fainted in pain. 'Poor thing, she nearly had her finger off.' I had a bandage around my bony finger. I was dreading how it would come out but it was alright.

At 18 years old I left the mill to start a new life of my own, I married and had 8 children, they go to a mill but they aren't orphans so they come back home at night.

*Belinda Forde (10)*
*Yarnfield Primary School*

# A Day In The Life Of Orphan Mary

I woke up at 5am every day. Around me I saw six beds, with some more girls sharing beds, about 16 girls. 'They all must be orphans too,' said Mary to herself because she had to whisper so no one could hear what she was saying.

What I get for breakfast is porridge and bread and water, I found it quite nice.

After breakfast I would go back and work in the horrible mill. Picking cotton from the dirty floor, mend broken threads, fix bobbins, clean machines. It is hard work for me.

My friends tell me what to do when I get stuck, they must be the only friends I have ever had. My friends are very nice to me. My best friend is called Annie, my other two friends are called Jessica and Rosie.

I feel OK, I have friends, I get good food, I guess I may say this life is OK. I may be tired and exhausted but I have friends.

At 7pm I get my evening meal, I get pork or bacon, milk or water. But I only get one of each.

Then I go to school for one hour. For Sunday dinner I get beef and a nice big mug of tea.

Finally, I go back to the dormitory in the big huge house and fall asleep as I am exhausted. About seven years to go.

*Robert Harper (10)*
*Yarnfield Primary School*

## A Day In The Life Of A Victorian Orphan

My name is Mary Scott. I was an orphan at 11 years old when my mother and father died. I am lonely and I am poor. I don't have any clothes or any food. I have to work all day. I have 2 frocks, 2 aprons, 2 vests and 2 pairs of stockings. I don't have time to play with my friends, I only have time to play with my friends on Sunday.

Each morning I wake up at 5 o'clock and I wash my face, get changed, have my breakfast and go off to work at quarter to six. I am so tired after work and my work starts at 6 o'clock in the morning and it finishes at 7 o'clock at night.

During the day I work. I put new bobbins on, mend broken threads, pick cotton from the floor and brush the machines. It is hard to brush machines.

For lunch I have pork or bacon and for a drink I have milk or water. I have not got money to buy lots of food. I don't have the best meal everyday, I only have the best meal on a Sunday. I have beef and a mug of tea on Sunday.

At the end of the day I go to school and play with my school friends. I have fun on Sundays because I play with my friends and have the best meal.

My favourite day is Sunday because I play with my friends, have the best, lovely, nice meal ever and have a restful and peaceful day. My friend is called Annie and she is poor like me and an orphan. She has to work and she is so kind.

*Shahara Choudhury (10)*
*Yarnfield Primary School*

## A Day In The Life Of...

One day there was a little girl called Zara, she wanted a rose and that's all she ever asked for, since they were very poor it would be very special to her. There were no flowers in the village they lived in, she hated it there because everyone was rude.

She lived next door to an old man, he was a very grumpy man and he didn't like people being polite to him and Zara didn't know, Zara was very polite and she said to him, 'Nice day isn't it, Mr Simons?'
He replied to her, 'Shut up and go away, I do not like answering little children like you!'
Zara did not like his attitude so she said, 'I'm sorry to say, but I do not like you being rude. You are very nasty!'
She ran home crying and he shouted, 'I don't care if you're crying, I'm on to you!' (still shouting).

She ran into her back garden and sat on the step and cried. Zara begged her Mum to move, all she said was, 'We can't move because we haven't got enough money.' She had to cry herself to sleep. The thing was she had to sleep on the floor. Her mum told her not to cry.

The next day she woke up and looked out of her window. She couldn't believe what she saw growing in Mr Simon's garden. She said to herself, 'It's . . . it's a rose!'

She ran downstairs as merry as the richest girl in the world, she flung open the door and guess what - nothing was there! She ran upstairs and screamed, 'Ah, ah, ah, ah, ah!'

Zara opened her window and threatened to jump out of her window, she was sitting on the ledge, her mum ran upstairs and said, 'Zara! Get off the ledge.'
She screamed, 'I'm not getting of till I get my rose!' Her mum calmed her down and she climbed back in.

Her mum said, 'I know you want a rose but I've only just found out the flowers don't grow in this village!'
She replied, 'So you are saying that no flower has ever grown here, not even a petal?'

She said, 'No and no flower ever will.'
Zara went, 'Oh.'
She walked upstairs shut the door, sat on the floor and cried, 'Wah, wah, wah!'
Her mum came up the stairs once again and said, 'What's the matter?'
Zara replied, 'I can't see a rose and when I thought I saw one it was my imagination, do you know what that feels like?'
'Well no' mum answered.

It come to night time and her mum made up a story that one day they would be rich. Zara made a wish before she went to sleep. She had a dream that the next day she would be rolling in money. Zara woke up and said, 'Same old thing, same old thing.'
Zara went down half asleep and her mum said, 'Look at all this money Zara!'
Zara replied, 'Oh, yeah, yeah, money!' She jumped and she ran.
Mum said, 'We could buy a new house and you could have as many roses as you like.'
She went, 'Ah cool!'
'Mum do you think we would be able to move with all this money.'
'Yes I suppose so!'

But guess what, she was dreaming, she woke up and said, 'I wish that was real.' It was all the same as usual. Zara found out that Mr Simons was a monster and he was growing a rose in his house that he's been treasuring for years, he had it before he moved to this village.

One day Mr Simons was so happy he invited Zara in, she just glared at the rose and she walked up to it, she was feeling naughty and she touched the rose and ran off. The next day Mr Simons turned into a monster and he had noticed that his rose had gone.

He ran to Zara's house. Zara said, 'I haven't seen your beautiful rose anywhere Mr Simons. Why what's happened.'
'Someone's nicked my rose!' he replied.
Zara said, 'How come you're a monster.' Trying to make conversation.
'You've got my rose haven't you?' He asked in a deep voice.
Zara replied, 'Maybe I have, but I really want a rose.'
The monster said, 'Well I really want it back!'

She ran and ran until she got to her aunty's house, she knocked with the rose in her hand, then the monster vanished because all the petals fell off and he was never seen again.

Roses grew everywhere because of what happened and Zara was really rich. It was all a dream telling her not to show off in front of people just because you're rich. You're meant to say, 'How does it feel to be poor?'

*Vicky Sheridan (9)*
*Yarnfield Primary School*

# A Day In The Life Of A Victorian Orphan

My name is Mary Scott, my mum and dad died when I was 11 years old. So I am an orphan. I work in a mill, I have a friend called Annie. We are best friends.

Each morning I wake up at 5.00am. I have to start my tasks at 6.00am with Annie it is fun a bit. At 5.00am I get dressed until I have to do my tasks.

During the day I pick up cotton from the floor, brush the machines at night, I have to do it for a week, it is quite boring.

For lunch I have porridge and bread for breakfast and pork or bacon with potatoes for dinner, I had milk and water for a drink.

At the end of the day I go to school in the evening and when I come back I go to bed and fall fast asleep, thinking about the day and what a good time I have had.

My favourite day is a Sunday because we get to play with friends and get the best dinner on Sundays. On Sundays we can do lots of stuff, it is fun on Sundays.

*Cherrelle Foster (10)*
*Yarnfield Primary School*